ANCIENT ORIGINS:

GENERATIONS

By CJ Bolyne

Also by CJ Bolyne:

The Trinity Trilogy:

Book 1: Trinity

Book 2: Anords Tyranny

Book 3: Guardians: Victory or Defeat

***

***

Ancient Origins: Generations

Copyright © 2016 C.J.Bolyne

Published by Cluster Publishing

ISBN: Ebook – 978-0-9879625-8-4

ISBN: Paperback – 978-0-9879625-7-7

Cover designed by Treaba Vasile

ACKNOWLEDGMENTS

Dedicated to the one person who encouraged me to pursue writing. Thank you Heather.

VAMPIRES

We all think we know every story and myth surrounding this particular subject; such myths like, they can't stand the sunlight, garlic makes them cringe or even burns them, the sight of a cross makes them hide their eyes and scream in fear, making them submit to the bearer of it, or that the feel of holy water splashed on them burns their already-dead skin.

Then there are the various ways of how to kill them: a stake through the heart, although, wouldn't that kill anyone? Or forcing them into the sunlight to burn to ash; cutting off their heads; the ever-popular silver bullet, although perhaps that applies only to the werewolf instead. Some stories tell of one vampire killing another, usually in the traditional way of the savage bite to the neck.

The traditional legend of the vampire starts with Vlad the Impaler, Prince of Wallachia who died in 1476 in Bucharest, Romania. The reported horrible atrocities he committed to his enemies and to his own people will forever be burned in our history. However, the legend is just that – a legend, made up by people who feared Vlad so much that when he died, people were convinced he may return to take revenge on any who opposed him. And perhaps he did! It was said that he found the secret to immortality – a secret he spent years searching answers for – –and that he still walks among us today.

This is not the case.

Some say vampires are born of the devil, others say that they are not of this world and most of us have no idea where they came from, but I will tell you the truth.

My name is Carlynn Willows and I want to tell you the real story of vampires – where they came from and who they are. I hope you're ready for this.

GENESIA

The court room was already filled to capacity, yet more spectators were pushing to get in. They had to see, had to witness the final verdict of the trial of the century.

There hadn't been a murder in fifty years. They had finally eradicated most crimes and then this happened. One of their own found dead, horribly mangled by this murderer. A young man whom no one would have ever expected to commit such an atrocity. He was the son of one of their own; the son of a supreme judge.

Valan and Nemar Kanor sat quietly in the front row of the court room awaiting the verdict. Valan could not preside over the case with the rest of the supreme judges because it was his own son on trial. Because, of course, it was the ruling of the other judges that his judgment would be 'clouded' and he had to admit, they were of course right. He looked over to his son, locked in the defendant cube, held in place with titanium shackles. His son looked back; such sadness in his expression. '*The fight in him is gone*,' Valan thought. He knew in his bones something had been wrong with the trial. The witnesses' testimonies were … too rehearsed, too perfect; and their demeanor while on the stand was nervous. Yet no one challenged their statements and not one of the representatives for his son tried to cross examine, stating that they had no questions for the witness.

Every time Valan tried to intervene, to help his son, the supreme judges silenced him saying that his thoughts and feelings were compromised.

The supreme judges stepped through the door of their private chambers behind the bench and took their seats.

"Silence," the Voicer, a guard and speaker for the judges, called out.

The room fell silent. To say you could hear a pin drop was an understatement. The Voicer approached the bench where the judges sat, reached out and took the verdict from one of them. He stepped back, faced the defendant, "Varian Kanor – rise," he ordered. The defendant did as he was ordered.

"Varian Kanor," he continued, "you have been accused of and judged for the murder of Gengie Daj. Our supreme judges have deemed you GUILTY. You are sentenced to the Alpha Penal Colony where you will spend the rest of your existence."

There was a collective gasp from the court room.

Varian was stunned and devastated at the same time. They wouldn't do that to him! Surely his friends would come forward and proclaim his innocence!

The Voicer approached the defendant cube, lowered the invisible security field surrounding Varian and grabbed hold of his wrist shackles. Varian winced. As he was being dragged through the back door of the court room, Varian called out, "Baxor, please tell them the truth!" but his voice was difficult to hear over the roar of the crowd. Some cheered that the murderer was getting what he deserved while others shouted and screamed in protest of the verdict.

Baxor kept his head bent so he wouldn't have to look at his best friend being sent to Alpha. It was harsh, but what else could he do? The others did the same – Jez, Kaeton and Madoc. The five had been close friends since childhood but Varian and Baxor were the best of friends. They did everything together, told each other everything, got into trouble together, covered for each other, etc., but now he couldn't help Varian and the others wouldn't either, not if they knew what was good for them.

Valan, holding his wife close to him, rose and quietly left the court room. At least they would let them see his son before he was sent away. This he knew; it was a wish always granted to the families before sentence was carried out. He had granted it many times in the hundreds of years he had been supreme judge. It had been so many years since a sentence like this was last handed down and he was the one who gave it. That was fifty years ago and now he would have to say goodbye to his only son, forever. No one was ever allowed to see the convicted felon again; no communication, nothing. It was considered part of the punishment, but that punishment extended to the family and friends left behind. In the minds of Genesians, if one of your own was sent to the Alpha Penal Colony, your family, and possibly friends, would suffer social implications. It was as if the family itself was blamed for the crime committed. Valan had to admit to himself, he had done the same to others in the past and now, it had come back to haunt him.

Surely there was something he had to do! This was wrong! Varian was innocent and he was going to prove it, one way or another.

Dusk came the next morning as usual. Valan and Nemar were mentally exhausted. They didn't bother going to rest the previous day with obviously too much on their minds. What would they say to their son whom they would see for the very last time?

They arrived at the station minutes before Varian would be escorted into the transport. Nemar held her son tightly, expressing her undying love, telling him she would never forget and asking him to do the same. Valan embraced his son, "I will never stop until I find out who did this to you Varian," he whispered in his ear, "be safe, stay alive until I can come for you. Promise me."

Varian promised and as the Voicer took his arm he said, "Baxor, father." Valan was about to ask his son why Baxor but the Voicer held his hand up to silence him, "You're done," he said and the door closed behind them.

Valan and Nemar stood watching as their only son disappeared, never to be seen again, possibly…

1

CARLYNN WILLOWS

I have to admit, I hated living in the country for the balance of my growing years. I was small for my age. I had dirty blond hair with a natural curl that was my bane in later years. I have big blue eyes, but not the pretty pale blue. Rather a darker blue that my mother said could change colour depending on my mood. Secretly, I wished I had green eyes. I had found an old photo of my grandmother who died when I was only two months old, and she had the most beautiful big green eyes that I couldn't help but stare at for long periods.

'Why can't my eyes be that pretty?'

I was born and lived the first years of my life in Winnipeg, Manitoba. Yep, I'm Canadian-born and a city kid. We lived on 288 Devon, a typical street with a small back yard that had the biggest crab apple tree I'd ever seen. All the neighbours knew each other.

I remember climbing that tree almost to the top, looking down and thinking, *'hmmmm that's a little too high'* and, of course, my mother would freak, yelling for me to climb right now down before I fell! The rest of our back yard was a small cul-de-sac with a few houses lined on each side. My friends and I played on the street constantly. Being a small street, the traffic was minimal.

Then the day came when my mother sat me down and told me we were moving to the country. I have to admit that I was devastated. I couldn't believe my ears! The country! I had to leave all my friends, my school and my street. THIS was my home. I guess I was in denial for a long time because I didn't inform my teacher at school that I was moving until two weeks before the big day. Needless to say, she was not impressed with me, but she got over it soon enough. I'm sure she saw it in my face that I was not happy about it but she did her best to comfort me and assure me that it would be fine. '*Yeah right*,' I thought.

Then moving day came. Ugh. Driving down a lonely dirt road that seemed to never end but, of course, it eventually did. It actually came to a dead end and to the east of the dead end was what looked like a long trail. At the end of that trail I saw an old two-story house and a few other smaller, equally old buildings. I guess that was our new home. It might as well have been at the end of the world; I imagined that if I'd taken a few more steps, I'd have fallen off. The nearest neighbour was half a mile away and they were ancient, or so I thought at my young age. The closest town was about two miles away; one of those tiny ones that you would miss if you blinked while driving through. It was called Sarto and had a small Ukrainian population of maybe ten?

There was nothing else there, just bush and forest for as far as I could see. I had an instant dislike for my new home. And it wasn't just that I was dropped into an environment I was completely new to, but something about the place gave me the creeps. As we drove up the long trail that was our driveway, that eerie feeling grew. I didn't understand it then but now I know the feeling was Deja-vu. I had the feeling that I had been there before, yet I knew that I hadn't. There were things I seemed to know about my new home, but how could I when I knew that this was the first time I had been here? At nine years old, this really freaked me out, to say the least.

My parents bought an old house and moved it onto an existing foundation after having the initial dilapidated house removed. We had to wait a few days before the electricity was hooked up and, without power, the toilet wouldn't work, so we had to use an outhouse … for god's sake! Although my dad fixed up the outhouse a little, I just hated going out in the dead of night. It was like we were pioneers again!

The house definitely needed work but that would come as the years went by. There was also an old log cabin on the property and I swear it was at least a hundred years old. There were two other small barns that both leaned a little to the right, looking as though they could topple at any second. They were not as old as the log cabin, I'm sure, and certainly not built like the log cabin either. My parents had to install support beams in both buildings, straightened them and fixed them up. One was converted into a small workshop for my dad, who liked to tinker with machinery and build things. He was kind of a jack-of-all-trades but his main ambition was to be a farmer. The other building was used as a garden shed and storage for the surplus of vegetables we harvested from our huge garden every fall. PS: I never want to weed a garden again! After we cleaned up the log cabin, it was used as a kind of summer kitchen and a hangout for my parents and their friends on summer evenings. It turned out pretty good and it still stands to this day. People sure knew how to build things back then.

The one thing I knew in my gut is that I had been there before and that made me feel afraid. I took a stroll on the huge yard one hot summer day and, believe me, those summers were bloody hot. About five hundred yards south of our house was a brush line and I was walking towards it knowing, for some reason, what was behind that brush. I knew, yet I kept going, telling myself, '*you're wrongc, you're wrong, this is just your imagination.*' The edge of the brush line was so close and I kept going, not really sure what was pulling me there – curiosity or maybe I just had to prove myself wrong.

I wasn't.

There it was – an old junk pile used as a garbage dump. That did it. I officially hated my new home. My parents tried their best to help me adjust but couldn't understand why I hated it so much in the country and how could a nine-year-old explain to her parents that she'd been there before. They'd think I was nuts or just a kid with an overactive imagination and would never take me seriously, so I never did explain. I was afraid to.

FALLING STARS

A year had gone by and it was summer once again. I had ceded to the fact that this was now home and I had to make the best of it. I did have to admit that it was certainly peaceful at night. The lightening bugs came out, flitting like tiny little strobe lights. I quite enjoyed watching them. You could hear crickets chirping, frogs croaking and the whippoorwills calling. My mother taught me a kid's song about the whippoorwills that I still remember today.

One hot summer night, not being able to sleep – we didn't have air conditioning yet – I stood by my bedroom window on the second floor, hoping for a breeze, when I looked up at the night sky. In the city, you didn't see the stars nearly as clearly and brightly as you do in the country. It was a beautiful sight. Now was also the very first time I had ever seen a falling star. It streaked across the sky so bright ... and it seemed so close. Was it supposed to be so close? How was I to know? The star didn't disappear in the sky either, but rather it seemed to disappear behind the trees on our land. I didn't hear an impact sound or feel the ground shaking. It was weird. Maybe it wasn't a star after all. Maybe it was a comet. Either way, I knew what I wanted to do in the morning – go out and see if I could find whatever it was that fell from the sky and landed on our property.

I awoke the next morning eager to start out on my hike in the bush so I could find the object that fell from the sky the night before.

I ran down the stairs, headed for the entrance and

started putting on my sneakers when I heard my mother call out, "Carlynn, where are you going?"

"I want to go out in the bush out back to look for something," I answered.

"Not before you eat your breakfast young lady," she said, "come on, get in here and eat." I complied begrudgingly, '*I don't have time for this*,' I thought. The milk and cereal were already on the table with an empty bowl and spoon waiting for me. I poured the cereal and ate as fast as I could. "Slow down," mom said, "you're going to choke."

I nodded but I couldn't slow down. I was on a mission and eating this cereal was slowing me down.

I finished my breakfast as quickly as I could, cleaned up my dishes, and put the cereal and milk away. "Now can I go?" I asked mom.

"Yes dear," she answered, "what's your hurry anyway?"

"I saw a falling star last night and I swear it landed on our land!" I answered excitedly.

Mom smiled and laughed to herself. "Okay, you go find your star, but be careful. Remember that a lot of the land in the back is swamp. You never know what holes you'll find and I don't want you to get hurt. You have half an hour and I want to see you back on the yard."

Half an hour! That wasn't enough time! "Ah, mom," I whined, "give me at least an hour, please?" and the pouted mouth formed with the wide begging eyes.

She sighed, "Ok, one hour and I expect to see your curly mopped head back in the front yard."

"Ok," I quickly agreed and ran out the door. I wasn't about to bargain for any more time or she wouldn't let me go at all. My mom sure liked to play hard ball that way.

I ran across the yard yelling, "Come on Jake!" I called out to my dog. He was a beautiful dog of mixed breed. I could almost ride him, he was so big, with longer chocolate brown fur. I always thought he was a shepherd-collie mix, but most people – even my parents – thought he had a bit of wolf in him. He was my protector. I recall playing in the field not far from our house when a rather large grey dog appeared out of nowhere, baring his teeth, growling and inching toward me when Jake jumped in front of me. He bared his teeth, growled and barked ferociously at the grey dog, and lunged toward him making it back off. It eventually turned and ran away. When I told my parents what had happened, their first reaction was to never let me leave the yard again. However, they relented when they saw that such a rule would never work on me so my dad said, "Ok, whenever you want to go away from the house, to the field or in the bush, you have to take Jake with you."

Mom wanted to protest but dad told her, "She's finally adjusting to country life, hon. We have to give her some space." Mom agreed, apprehensively. I know she worried constantly.

I half ran, half skipped across the yard into the field and headed for the trail that led into the bush. Jake happily running beside me, barking excitedly. When we entered the bush, I said, 'Ok Jake, let's see if we can find the falling star!'. He whined and cocked his head, you know how dogs do?

I'm not sure how far we went, pushing underbrush aside and bending branches, just to get through the dense bush, when Jake barked and ran ahead of me.

"Jake!" I called and ran after him. He hadn't gone very far – just about a hundred yards or so – when I found him in a small clearing pacing around a hole in the ground. It was a pretty big hole too, 'Wow, dad's truck could fit in that hole,' I said to myself. "Jake, come here boy," I called to him and he came quickly to my side. "Maybe this is one of those sinkholes mom and dad are always talking about," I said to Jake. Being my closest friend, I always talked to him, even if he didn't understand.

Standing at the edge of the hole, I estimated it to be about six feet deep, but what did I know? I was only ten years old. Jake was sure acting funny though, leaning against me like he wanted to push me away from it, whining. "Shhh, Jake," I said, "I just want to see … it's no big deal. Relax. Sit." I commanded. He sat instantly but still whined and his front paws padded the ground impatiently. I knew he didn't like it here but I wasn't about to turn and walk away. I saw something fall last night and I wanted to know what it was.

Peeking over the edge, I saw nothing. Great, no comet to bring back and show mom. It was a weird hole though. The walls were smooth like it had been cut into the ground. The only part that wasn't smooth was the 'floor' of the pit. The dirt was disturbed, – not smooth.

Now Jake started barking wildly. "Jake, cool it!" I said, but it was useless. He wasn't listening. I followed his gaze to see what the problem was, maybe another wolf, a bear or raccoon. You just never knew in these parts. I saw movement coming from behind a small bush.

"Hello," I called out, "is anyone there?" No one answered and the rustling immediately stopped. Ok, I knew enough by now to know that if there was an animal behind the bush, it wouldn't freeze as soon as it heard a voice. Either I'd hear it running away or it would come out into the open. Especially if it thought I was a potential meal.

"Um, whoever you are, I'm leaving. I guess you want to be left alone, I get it," I called out. Still no response. "Come on, Jake," I patted his large head, turned and walked away. I was also a little freaked out, to be honest.

When we were far enough away from the hole and I was sure we couldn't be seen, we ducked behind the trees and peeked through the small branches. "Look!" I whispered to Jake.

There was someone there! It was not an animal but a

person. What the heck is he doing on our land? Or was it a woman? It was difficult to tell. The person had shoulder length black hair, so black that when the sun hit it, it had a blue hue and he – or she – wore a full length gray, almost silver, cloak. My view was partially blocked by branches and leaves. I tried to push a leaf aside quietly so as not to alert the stranger that I really had not left the scene. But by then, he or she was gone, "Ok Jake, let's go." I said. "Whoever it was is gone now."

As I rose, Jake started growling, "What now?" I asked him, but I saw the answer. The stranger we had seen was a man and he was now standing right behind me. "Oh," was all I could muster.

No matter how scared I am or was, I've never been a screamer. In fact, I become just the opposite. I'd clam up, not able to speak, squeak, yell, or scream. I backed away, taking Jake with me, who was still growling, and we spun and ran as fast as we could. Jake never ran ahead of me, but always stayed behind to make sure he could protect me. We made it to the edge of the bush, with the field before my house ahead of us. It was the first time since we'd moved here I was truly glad to see it. "Jake, come," I ordered and we raced across the open field toward the yard, not stopping until we reached the large deck. Exhausted, I flopped down panting, with Jake beside me giving me his sloppy kisses, "yeah, yeah, Jake," I reassured him and gave him a big hug. "You really are my protector, aren't you?" His answer was to give me more sloppy kisses.

3

TEN YEARS LATER

I miss Jake and guess I always will. He died about a year ago while I was away at university. My father called me the day it happened. He was mowing the lawn one afternoon when a bear wandered on to the yard and was heading for him. Dad thought the animal was probably rabid. Jake, being older already, was still the valiant defender and positioned himself between the bear and my dad. I stopped my dad from telling me the rest. By now, I could guess and was already crying. Dad assured me he gave Jake the best burial and even put a stone up for him. Mom and dad always said Jake was special.

I never did mention the discovery Jake and I made on the farm to my parents. Perhaps I was a little paranoid, but I didn't want to open myself up to ridicule or teasing and I certainly didn't want my parents overreacting. And they may have stopped me from going into the bush ever again.

Speaking of ridicule or teasing, that was exactly what happened to me in middle school. I befriended a girl named Ellen. She was the first person who gave me the time of day and didn't ostracize me because I wasn't born in the area.

I thought that we got along quite well, especially for the first few weeks. In fact, I became comfortable enough to call her my best friend. My parents were thrilled, "Carlynn finally has friends!" I overheard mom say.

One Monday morning though, with a fresh week of school about to begin, I was heading to my locker when

Jason, one of the boys in my class, came up behind me. "Hey Carlynn, see any falling stars lately? Or maybe strangers in the bush?" He walked into class laughing, with several of his cronies following him. I was the last one into the classroom and that's when the laughing, throwing wads of paper, and name calling began. Thankfully, the teacher quieted everyone down and class began. Ellen sat in front of me. She turned, looked me straight in the eye and said, "Freak." I never spoke to her again. As it turned out, after a few weeks, I didn't have to see any of them again. It had been discovered that I was gifted, and my parents informed me and that, given this new situation at my current school, they thought it would be best if they sent me to a school for advanced children.

I have to admit, I was mind numbingly bored with public school and the reason was, as I was told, I was not being challenged in my classes.

It was the best thing that ever happened to me. I never looked back. I was surrounded by kids with the same intellectual ability as I had and I found it refreshing, plus I was away from the hell I experienced in the old school.

Now, here I am all grown up, same curly dirty blond

hair, same dark blue eyes, ivory complexion with a few freckles I hoped would eventually disappear but didn't, the slim build I inherited from my mother thank goodness, and about five feet six inches tall. Taller than my family thought I'd be. My mother always called me beautiful but she's my mom. All children are beautiful in their mother's eyes, aren't they?

I had just graduated from university along with several other of the 'gifted' ones, with degrees in anthropology, archeology and ancient history. I know that these professions were not considered the norm for gifted students, but I always felt different anyway. My parents wanted me to be a scientist and become famous for curing diseases such as cancer, aids, etc., which are all good causes, but medicine just didn't interest me.

I wanted to study the "who, what, where and whys" of the human race. Why we're here, where we came from, how we evolved to where we are. The many different cultures, religions and so on. I even went on a few digs while still a student and not just in the obvious places like Egypt or China, but in more remote areas and less interesting to others, such as Romania, Ireland, Scotland

and even Australia. Yes, I was a busy student and loved every minute of it.

University was also where I met my now closest friends, Lynn, Rae and Jade.

I met Lynn Connor the first day in admissions. We chatted a little in the lineup and quickly learned that we were taking the same courses so we ended up sitting together in our first class of the semester. Neither of us knew anyone else so it stands to reason we would sit together and, as a result, we became fast friends. It turned out that she was also part of a 'gifted' class and we shared the same interests.

Lynn was born in London, England and her family moved to Canada when she was ten years old. I could still detect a faint English accent in her voice. Her parents weren't rich, but they worked hard and Lynn had to put herself through school. Her parents barely managed to pay for the special school she attended as a youngster but when it came time for her to go to university, they sadly informed her they couldn't afford it and she'd have to do it on her own if she wanted to go. She worked as a waitress and took extra shifts whenever she could and she always made great tips. She knew how to work a table, was always polite, and went out of her way to make sure the customer was happy with their meal and service. It didn't hurt that she was very cute. Petite at five foot three inches, with long strawberry blond hair, big blue eyes that you swear could look right through you, with dark lashes, and a great figure that could rock a mini skirt. I have to admit that I was quite jealous of her looks for a long time, especially because she didn't have to wear a stitch of makeup and would still look great. Let me tell you, there was such a thing as natural beauty when it came to Lynn Connor. The only time we could swap clothing was when one of her tops shrunk in the laundry and no longer fit her. With her being a little larger in the chest than I, she gave me that top and said, "Here, it shrunk in the dryer. It's too tight over the boobs!" She'd laugh, handing it to me and I'd laugh and say, "bitch." It was a private joke between us. Although we were the same size in jeans, I was three inches taller so that didn't work at all.

We met Rae and Jade Hill in the University cafeteria a week after the semester started.

They were identical twins, about the same height as

me, with long dark poker straight hair, dark brown, almost black eyes, lashes to match and olive skin. They had an exotic beauty to them. They should have had men crawling all over them.

The cafeteria was packed, with the exception of their table where there were two seats left. Lynn and I approached the table, with our trays in hand and asked them if we could sit. The two looked up in unison and nodded. We sat down. Rae and Jade smiled at each other. Ok, this was a little weird, were they secretly laughing at us? This was my paranoia coming to the surface again, "What's so funny?" I asked.

Rae was the first to respond, "Nothing. I'm Rae and this is Jade," she said pointing at an obvious identical twin. Jade smiled.

"Um, I'm Carlynn and this is Lynn," I said, still uncomfortable with their previous smile to one another.

Lynn and I shifted in our seats a bit, then proceeded to eat lunch in silence.

"We're sorry," Jade spoke up, "we don't mean to be rude, but it's just that most people don't want to sit with us, so when you asked to join us, we were glad to have the company."

"Ah, cool," Lynn said.

I smiled on the surface, secretly reprimanding myself for my insecurities. We ate our lunch, sat back and enjoyed the latte we both had, idle chit chat being the conversation of the hour. A few minutes before class was starting for the afternoon, I worked up the courage to ask, "Why don't most people want to sit with you two?"

"We're different," Rae responded, "I guess too different for most."

"Don't most twins have a unique bond?" Lynn asked, "Or so I've heard and read studies on it."

"That's the common perception but ours is more unique than others," Rae said.

"Shhh," Jade said, "remember what happened the last time?" she quietly reminded Rae.

"Sorry," Rae apologized, "I tend to talk too much, at least Jade thinks so anyway. Oh, we're going to be late for class!" The two grabbed their books, said their goodbyes and darted off, leaving Lynn and I baffled at the uninformative conversation we just had with them.

"Ok, that was weird," Lynn said.

"Yep, sure was," I responded, "there's something about those two that is different, strange even, and I think...there's a story there."

"Here we go again," Lynn rolled her eyes.

AFTER GRADUATION

After graduation, Lynn, Rae, Jade and I took a backpacking trip to Europe. We had it planned a year before we graduated. It was a gift from our parents with the exception of Lynn. She worked for the cash to take the trip and politely refused any help from the rest of us.

"It's a gift Lynn," I told her.

"Thanks, but no thanks," she replied, "I appreciate the thought though."

That was the end of it. Rae, Jade and I shrugged, "Ok," the twins said, "have it your way."

We always find it kind of eerie the way Rae and Jade could speak in unison.

We had a blast touring Europe. Our first stop was France, of course, then Spain, Italy, Germany, and Austria.

Paris, the famous city of love – not that we found love, mind you – then Spain with such a colourful culture and wonderful beaches. Italy was one of my favourites, with the Coliseum, Roman Forum, St. Peter's Basilica, the Pantheon and the Vatican. Pictures are one thing, but when you see these sites for real, it is truly awe inspiring.

Germany and Austria were wonderful too; the architecture in the old world simply can't be beat. We even toured through what was left of one of the concentration camps from World War II. Not the best idea we had. Seeing the large buildings where people were kept in conditions worse than one would keep their farm animals, ovens where humans were burned; sometimes alive, and a mountain of shoes taken from these poor innocent men, women and children. By the time the tour ended, Rae and Jade were both particularly upset when they spotted a pair of baby booties within the pile of old shoes. We couldn't get out of there fast enough.

On the tour bus, the twins sat quietly, holding hands while tears streamed down their cheeks. Lynn and I were also weepy, "You two going to be ok?" I asked. They nodded.

After an hour long ride back to the tourist centre, we got off the bus and started down the street.

"Quietest bus I've ever been on," Lynn half whispered.

"Yeah," was all I could say.

The next day we were on the road again and managed to hitch several rides on our way back to Paris. It didn't hurt that we were four girls with the Canadian maple leaf on our jacket. We'd elect whose turn it was to stick out her thumb, and boom ... a car always stopped. I must say, the people we met were wonderful and always obliging.

Back in Paris, we booked ourselves into the 5-star La Maison Champs-Elysées. It was agreed between us that we'd stay at a classier hotel before going home on our last night in Europe.

Although we were kind of getting used to the youth hostels and shelters, this was a great hotel! We had a large beautiful suite with two king size beds, a small kitchenette, a lounging area with a massive black leather sectional and a fifty-inch TV. The powder room was like a mini spa. Needless to say, we squealed like little school girls when we saw it.

I took my time getting ready for our final night of club hopping. We all donned our minis, tight tops and high heels – couture we were saving for the last night of partying. Our intention was to get plastered and dance the night away.

5

OUR LAST NIGHT

The door man slash bouncer opened the rope to let the four of us into the club. The place was bouncing with loud music and dancing, sweaty people doing the latest moves. The bar was buzzing with line ups five people deep. It was going to be a challenge getting a drink, never mind finding a free table we could stake a claim on.

"There!" Rae shouted over the pounding music, pointing to a small table only a few feet from the bar.

"Quick, grab it!" Jade said.

The two pushed their way through the crowd to reach the table. Rae got to it first and placed her hand on the table to claim it. At the exact same moment, another hand reached it. Jade was right behind Rae, with Lynn and myself following. We gathered around it. "I got here first." Rae informed the stranger.

"I beg to differ." he replied.

"We can share." I uttered, grudgingly.

Rae sighed and rolled her eyes, "Fine."

The four now became five crowding around the tiny table. Luckily, we were able to flag down a waiter to take our drink orders. I was sipping my Bellini, savouring the strong peach flavour, scanning the dance floor. Lynn was dancing with a good looking local who hadn't waste any time asking her to dance. I turned back to comment on Lynn's good luck when I noticed the guy we were sharing our table with. I hadn't really looked at him before, but now something about him struck me. 'Oh no,' I thought, Deja vu again. My gut told me that we'd met before.

He smiled at me, with a too perfect mouth of straight pearly white teeth. He had dark hair, a bit on the long side, with a slight wave, and black eye lashes attached to equally black eyes. Most women would secretly curse a man with lashes like his and I did just that. He had those chiseled good looks, actually, he was freakin' hot! One thing I found peculiar was how flawlessly pale his skin was. I mean, I couldn't see one pore. It was almost like porcelain. Of course I was looking at him through the flashing lights of the strobe, a slight smoky haze in the air and the odd stage light streaking across my eyes. It was hardly the perfect environment to judge a person's looks in. Oh hell. Damn, he was hot!

After an hour of dancing with a few different guys, talking excitedly with the girls, Lynn and I decided to step outside for a breath of fresh air before we left for another hot spot. We weren't about to waste our last night at one place. But about twenty or so other people had the same idea. The back alley seemed almost as packed as the club. The narrow alley had others taking in the night air, cooling off and probably trying to sober up a bit.

Lynn and I stuck together, talking quietly, deciding

where to go next. We heard a familiar sound of someone getting sick and Lynn motioned to move farther away from the sound, "Ew," she whispered.

As we stepped aside, I accidently bumped into someone. It was him.

"Oh, hey, sorry about that." I apologized.

"It's ok." he said.

'*Alright,*' I thought, '*he IS hot.*' Seeing him in the glow of the street light confirmed that my first assessment of him was correct. '*Shit, why do I have to meet him on my last night in Paris!*' I asked myself.

"So," I said, trying to be polite, "what was your name again?"

VARIAN

"I never told you my name." he replied, rather too arrogantly. I hated that.

"Fine, be that way." I snapped.

He laughed and said, "Varian. My name is Varian." and the arrogance disappeared. I smiled and relaxed a bit.

"Varian. That's quite an unusual name ... Varian, I

like it. Is it Hungarian, or Russian?" My curiosity started to take over; Lynn nudged my ribs, reminding me to reel it in a little.

He smiled that perfect smile and said, "It is foreign, yes".

I returned a half-hearted smile, not looking him in the eye. Actually, it was really a smirk. Something about those eyes made me uncomfortable. It was like he could see right through me, like he knew my inner most thoughts and secrets. There was that uneasy silence in the air.

"You do not trust me." he stated.

My defenses were instantly up, "I don't know you." I replied. "One usually gets to know a person before one trusts said person!"

"I see." he said.

Condescending jerk! No matter, we were leaving for the next club.

Lynn, wanting to leave an awkward situation, said with a smile that didn't quite reach her eyes, "Ok, well, nice to meet you Varian, but we must be going. Thanks again for sharing the table. Bye now." She grabbed my arm and pulled me back into club.

"That guy gives me the creeps." she said, "Let's find the twins and go."

I nodded.

Rae and Jade were at our table, chatting with a couple of guys. They exchanged email addresses and said their goodbyes, Jade saying, "We'll never hear from them again." and Rae saying, "Don't be so pessimistic. You never know."

We hit two more clubs before dragging our tired, tipsy asses back to our hotel room. The flight home was early in the morning and it was to be an exhausting day with only two hours sleep that night.

Boarding the plane home, I had to admit that I was really looking forward to *being* home. Thankfully, it was still warm in Canada, but in a couple of months, the deep freeze would come. I had to laugh at myself – being born and raised on the prairies, yet I absolutely hated the extreme cold. I don't mind winter and snow, but I do mind those days when the mercury falls to minus 30 degrees Celsius and those blasted wind chills of minus 40 to 50. Good grief!

We settled into our first class seats – another luxury

we decided to treat ourselves with. We'd be in the air for approximately 11 hours and who wants to be in the crowded coach area? With Rae and Jade sitting in front of Lynn and I, Rae looked over the back of her seat, and was about to say something when she closed her mouth abruptly, turned and sat down again. We heard some whispering, then Jade peeked over her seat and quickly sat back down again. More whispering.

"Hey you two," I said, kneeing the back of Jade's seat, "what's going on?"

The whispering stopped and Jade looked over to me and said, "He's here." She sat down again.

"Who's here?" I asked, but got no answer. I looked at Lynn, she shrugged and said, "You lot are bonkers sometimes."

Lynn had a better view of the other passengers, being in an aisle seat. I've always loved the window seat. I get such a high when the plane speeds down the runway and lifts off the tarmac.

Lynn quickly scanned the plane looking for anyone familiar. After a few seconds she saw him.

"Bloody hell." she said to no one in particular.

"What?" I asked impatiently, at the same time noticing her British accent. It only returned when something bothered her.

"Lynn, what?" I asked again, exasperated.

She sat back quickly, pushing herself into the back of the seat, as if to hide.

"That bloke, uh, oh shit…that guy we met at the club in Paris, he's on the plane!" she said.

"Seriously? Varian?" I said, my tone doubtful, but her baby blues were as big as saucers, telling me she was a little freaked out.

It would be a few more minutes before take-off, so I decided to take a quick stroll toward the rear of the plane, pretending to look through the overhead compartments looking for my carry-on. That would give me a chance to see if I could spot him.

Yep, there he was, near the back of the first class section. I was relieved that he didn't seem to see me, but I was wrong. As I turned to head back, he did see me.

"Hello," he said.

"Hi," I said sharply and continued on. I sat down and Lynn asked, "So is it him?"

"Uh huh."

"What do you think he's doing here?" she asked.

"I don't know," I answered, "I didn't ask him."

"Weird," she said.

"Probably just a coincidence. We don't know where he's from. He may live in Canada too for all we know, or he's traveling; on vacation, who knows?" I'm not sure I was very convincing. My deja vu was bothering me and Lynn could see it.

"Yeah right," she replied, unconvinced.

Rae and Jade were listening, and they glanced at each other, turned and sat down again.

BACK HOME

We weren't home one week when the twins were called to work at the prestigious S.E.T.I. Institute – Search for Extraterrestrial Intelligence – in California. Jade called to deliver their good news. I offered my congrats to them and said how much I'd miss them. It made sense though, as they were astronomy majors and extremely gifted in that field.

I, on the other hand, was still waiting for answers from the various places to which I had applied. One of the drawbacks was my age. Being 21, I was perceived to be too young for potential employers. I had three degrees. Most people with the same education were pushing thirty and assumed to be more mature.

While waiting for responses, I decided to spend a week with my parents on the farm, enjoying the quiet and solitude. I found it so funny that, when I was young, I couldn't get away from the country fast enough and now, here I was and I didn't want to leave. Interesting how things change.

My parents got a new dog, too. He was a heeler/collie cross that dad named Duke. I'm sure it was after one of his favourite old western movie stars – dad had a corny side.

Duke was half the size Jake had been. He had longer hair like a border collie but the mottled colours of a heeler and, boy was he fast! He could run like a deer. Dad said, "I swear he's the reincarnation of Jake, he's very protective." I smiled, "well, we'll see," I responded, "I'm going to take a walk in the bush and Duke can come along." Dad nodded, smiled and off we went.

The bush was the same as I remembered when I was a kid. Duke walked by my side the whole time, '*Dad was right*,' I thought to myself. We ended up at the place I found years earlier. The fallen star. '*What drew me here*?' Something did and I suddenly knew the reason!

Varian! This is where I first saw him! That's why my meeting him in Paris bothered me so much! I was a child the first time we met and Varian was an adult. Now I'm an adult and Varian ... well, Varian hadn't changed at all. I sat down at the edge of the hole with my legs dangling over the edge. Come to think of it, the hole hadn't changed either. You'd think the grass would have grown in and the bush crept in at least a little. But it hadn't at all. Maybe it was because of radiation fallout from the star?

My cell phone suddenly rang, tearing me from my thoughts. I answered it and a strange man's voice asked, "Carlynn Willows?"

"Yes."

"This is Hugh Morgan. I work for a private institute of archeological studies in Winnipeg," he said, "We'd like you to come in Monday morning for a meeting."

"I'm sorry, who do you work for?" I asked.

"C.A.S.I.? The Centre of Archeological Studies Institute." he answered. "Perhaps you have heard of us?"

The name sounded familiar to me but I couldn't quite remember where I'd heard it.

"Ok, I'll be there. What time?" I asked.

"8 am."

After Hugh gave me the address to C.A.S.I. and gave me specific instructions on where to park, he ended the call saying, "I look forward to seeing you on Monday."

"Well Duke," I said, as I hung up, "I might just have a job prospect. I just don't remember applying to 'C.A.S.I.'" Duke licked my nose and I giggled.

Suddenly, a twig snapping in the woods stopped me mid giggle. Duke immediately started growling, but never left my side. I looked in the direction I heard the noise I thought it had come from but the bush was very dense so I couldn't see much. I stood up to get a better view and Duke moved in front of me. He was very protective. Just then, something caught my peripheral vision; it was something dark. Duke started barking wildly. This was

Deja vu all over again. Jake did the same thing so many years ago when I first came to investigate a falling star.

"Ok Duke," I grabbed his collar, "let's get out of here." I turned and ran from the hole, not stopping this time until I got to the edge of the bush. The open field and house in the distance was a comforting sight.

STAR STRUCK

'*Interesting human,*' Varian thought, as he approached the hole. '*Really still the same.*' He sat down beside it. He would have to wait till night fall. That would be in a few hours and he was getting hungry again. He hated the idea of hunting the wildlife in the area but he didn't have much of a choice; he had to eat. He detected a scent in the air – a deer, likely a buck. He took out his weapon of choice and followed the scent for a few seconds, "There you are," he whispered. The large buck didn't have a chance. Varian gave the blow that paralyzed the animal before moving in for the kill. He hated the taste, but it was food. After having his fill, he buried the carcass quickly and concealed the area with the broken twigs and leaves readily available on the ground.

Back at the hole, he sat as dusk started to fall, turning the smartphone in his hands as he waited.

Dusk turned to dark. The stars twinkled brightly as Varian searched for it. '*There*,' he thought, '*found you*.' He took a small triangular object out of his coat pocket and attached it to the back of the phone. '*Please work*,' he whispered.

9

C.A.S.I.

I arrived at a large building, seemingly made of glass. It was a beautiful sight, actually, and in the shape of Egypt's step pyramid. The entire facility was surrounded by a high voltage fence. I found that odd. Why would an archeological institute need this kind of security? And why are there armed guards at the gate? I deduced they must be storing historic artifacts they've found.

I managed to get past the guards who were waiting for me, with my name on their list of expected visitors. I parked where I was instructed to and headed for the only entrance I could find.

The reception area looked antiseptic. The walls were a stark white with no decorations such as paintings. There was no furniture at all; no chairs or tables. In fact, there was no waiting area at all. There was only one desk with a young woman sitting behind it, looking desperately bored. I checked in with her and she immediately picked up the phone to call Hugh Morgan.

Within minutes, a man appeared, about six feet tall, sandy brown hair, with a slightly receding hairline. I guessed him to be about 50 but handsome nonetheless. He introduced himself and escorted me to an equally antiseptic boardroom with a large oval oak table and twelve leather chairs surrounding it. 'Definitely need a decorator,' I thought.

Hugh motioned for me to have a seat. After a moment, the door opened and Lynn walked in, escorted by a very large, scary looking security guard.

"Lynn!"

"Carlynn! What are you doing here?" she asked.

"Mr. Morgan called me," I answered.

"Me too!" she said.

We smiled at each other. After another moment, the door once again opened; and in entered the twins. *'What the hell is going on?'* I thought, *'Rae and Jade are experts in astronomy, not archeology, AND they work for S.E.T.I. now.'*

Hugh waited for the rest to take their seats before he started, "Alright then. Now that we are all here, I am sure you are wondering why we have brought archeology together with astronomy," he began. Seeing the confusion on our faces, he smiled in an attempt to reassure us; it wasn't working well, in my opinion, but he continued. "We here at C.A.S.I. have been sending crews out to digs around the world. Every time we have heard of a farmer discovering a cache of bones that were exposed after a field has been cultivated, we send out a crew. Just recently, an Egyptologist has discovered a new tomb and the latest crew – you four –will be dispatched. To Romania. It seems that a curator of the old castle that was once inhabited by

Vlad the Impaler has accidently found a tunnel and he called our office. He has asked me to send some of our best to Romania to investigate."

"That's all great Mr. Morgan," I said, "for Lynn and I, but I fail to understand why Rae and Jade are here. They work for S.E.T.I and …"

"Yes, yes," he interrupted, "I know this is strange but the curator found carvings, among other things that do not add up. He brought in a local expert who is convinced those carvings, etc., are not human."

"You mean evidence of an extraterrestrial presence?" Jade said.

"Yes," Hugh answered.

"When do we leave?" Rae asked, excitedly.

"Hold on," Lynn said, "why the four of us? I mean, granted we are the best," she smiled, "but we have limited field work experience. We've only just graduated from university."

"Right you are," Hugh said, "but you are young enough to be open-minded. Most of our crew are older and are more reluctant to expand their way of thinking. They are more stuck in the old ways."

"So what makes you think we're more open to this concept than anyone else?" I asked.

"Hope," he answered. "Your youthfulness compels you to ask the hard questions and search for the answers, no matter what. Rae, Jade – you believe there is other life out there, do you not?" he asked, pointing upwards.

"We work for S.E.T.I.," Jade said, "I think that's a given."

"We've just recently expanded our search of the Keplar system, which is part of the Lyra constellation. We've also found a new cluster of galaxies in an area of space thought to be empty; with the help of the Hubble telescope!"

"But we've never received a response from space," Jade interjected, "We send out constant communication with no answer."

"Yet."

Jade glared at her sister for a second.

"Ok, ok, so how do we play into this?" I asked Hugh.

He answered, "You and Lynn are the diggers and Rae and Jade are the star gazers. Diggers find and analyze the time period. Star gazers check out those unusual symbols that should not be there. Ladies, we want to find out how long they have been here and where they came from, and ... find out if there are others," he concluded.

10

THE CONNECTION

The communication device worked like a charm. Varian knew the human race had evolved, but he was surprised at how far they had come.

"How are you doing, son?" his father asked.

"As good as can be expected," Varian answered, "I miss you and mother; I miss home."

Valan heard the despair and sadness in his son's voice.

"Have you any information on Baxor? He set me up father."

"I have been trying, son, but no one is talking. Every time I try to approach Baxor or any of the others, they run and the Voicer appears. He seems to be everywhere," Valan said, "I try to investigate more, check records and reports, but the high council, including the supreme judges, block me at every turn."

The signal was starting to break up, which meant the satellite was moving. "Father, please keep trying," Varian said.

"Varian, be careful," Valan warned his son, as the connection was breaking.

"Father!"

The signal was lost.

"Argh," he said, in frustration and punched the nearest tree, which fell over with a crash. He leaned against the tangled mass of roots that popped out of the ground from the massive blow, his breathing heavy. He was in this horrible prison because of a lie. How was he supposed to vindicate himself when he was so far from home? He had to rely on his parents, especially his father, who was being blocked at every turn. Plus, there were the social ramifications for them because of his imprisonment.

Ten years. He had been here for ten years and this was the first time he'd been able to talk to his father. A note and communication device was slipped into his prison uniform by his father the last time they hugged goodbye. No one noticed, not even the Voicer or himself.

It took this long for Earth's technology to catch up to a point where it could work. Earth was still primitive from a Genesian technological stand-point.

He would try again in twenty-four hours and hope his father would be there; perhaps mother too this time. He wanted to talk to his mother to see that she was alright and assure her he was well.

This so-called 'prison' was not what he expected. It was supposed to be very primitive, with monsters and danger around every corner. A place where the prisoners were hunted endlessly and had to fight to stay alive. These were the stories he'd heard his whole life and now that he was here, he realized those stories were wrong. Their information needed to be updated.

It wasn't too difficult to live here, really. One thing that is a hardship was time. Time goes by slowly here, but perhaps that is part of the sentence, that prisoners are forced to endure and the diet they have to resort to just to stay alive. '*They are just like the barbarians of their past; animals,*' Varian thought.

ROMANIA

"I can't believe we're going to Romania to investigate a myth!" I said, "And Vlad the Impaler? Really?"

"You know they say that myths or legends ring with truth," Lynn chimed in, "although they are often embellished more and more as time goes on and stories are repeated over and over." I rolled my eyes.

"Don't do that!" Lynn scolded.

"Sorry," I said, "I forgot your heritage is of the 'old world', but you have to admit it sounds a little far-fetched. I mean, we dig up bones, human or animal and analyze date, time, what they ate, how they lived and died. We've uncovered ruins of villages. This, this is investigating ET for Pete's sake!"

Jade interrupted, "Carlynn, think about it. With all the galaxies, millions of them, I might add, we've found many planets similar to ours. Do you really think Earth is the only planet that has intelligent life?"

"I … you have a point," I conceded.

The private jet taxied down the runway. My favourite part of flying – the takeoff.

The institute had its own jet which meant no more crowded airports or the invasive security check points. It had been only two weeks since they had all come home from Europe and now, here they were, on their way back.

The 17-hour flight was uneventful and we slept most of the time, recharging for the long days ahead of us.

Once the plane landed, we dragged our tired selves

off the plane and headed for customs. We went through with no fanfare, headed to the baggage claim, found our luggage and went to find a cab. To our surprise, there stood a tall thin man dressed in a chauffeur's suit holding up a sign with my name on it. Looks like we were getting the royal treatment!

The chauffeur loaded our bags in the trunk of the town car limousine and opened the door for us to get in. Once we were all seated, he closed the door and got into the driver's seat.

'*What a gentleman,*' I thought.

We drove for a few minutes when I noticed we were headed out of the city, "Aren't you going the wrong way?" I asked our quiet driver.

"No madam. I am ordered to drive you straight to castle Dracula", he answered.

"But our bags. We'd like to check into our hotels…"

"Not to worry madam. I will take care of that for you. The curator is waiting for you."

Once there, the curator, Mikhael, who initially found the 'secret' cave, led us up the long path to the infamous castle of Vlad the Impaler. Lynn and I had been in Romania once before during our years in college, but we never got the opportunity to investigate the large structure. "No time," our professor had said.

Mikhael led us down a long stone stairway that was every bit as eerie as it is in the movies. Rae and Jade whispered between themselves, "I don't like this part," Rae said.

"I know," Jade answered, "such sadness and suffering in these walls." We finally hit the bottom. It was obvious that it served as a dungeon/jail in medieval times. I found it strange and a little unsettling how things had been left virtually untouched since then. The unsettling part being the tools used to torture prisoners. The rack, used to stretch a person's limbs to the point of dislocation or even ripping the limb from the body. The elongate saw used to saw a body in half. Did I mention the victim was usually still alive? The head crusher, a device that really doesn't need further description. It makes a person shutter and be very grateful not to have lived in the 15th century. Is it morbid that I found this fascinating at the same time? Probably.

Vlad's legacy was that of a tyrant. A very different

description than before his battles against the Ottoman Empire. He was seen as a hero or saviour of Wallachia, protecting his homeland from the invaders, and using the most disturbing scare tactic one could use to intimidate the enemy. He impaled them by the thousands. It has been described as a forest of bodies, blood and, for those still alive when impaled, screams of agony.

He was finally captured and imprisoned by the Turks who ultimately beheaded him. A mercy in my opinion, as they could have tortured him in revenge for how their soldiers had died.

It is said that he is buried in a monastery, possibly at Comana, but this has been up for debate for many years as a body has never actually been found. This is, in part, why his castle was abandoned when stories started circulating that Vlad had returned. They say that he made a deal with the devil. A deal that let him live indefinitely, but immortality came at a cost; he would require the blood of humans. I suppose that, had I lived during that time in history, I may have run for the hills too. '*Good grief*,' I thought.

At the bottom of the stairwell, we came to a wall

and waited. The curator turned and said, "Ladies, I came upon this purely by accident." He kicked at a brick on the lower part of the solid wall. Upon closer inspection, I noticed that the brick was marked with white paint so it could be found again. Clever.

The wall opened inward, like you would expect any brick door to do, with one exception. It was completely silent. How can a brick wall move with absolutely no noise?

The curator smiled, "When I accidently 'kicked' the brick the first time, I didn't even notice the door open. I touched the brick with the back of my heel so my back was turned. Then I felt a draft," he said. He motioned for us to follow him. We entered a round room, about a thousand square feet in diameter.

"It's huge!" Rae gasped, "And you only found it a few weeks ago?" Jade finished for her sister.

"Yes," he answered.

He went around lighting the torches that had last been lit approximately 550 years ago and that were still in impeccable working form. They lit up the room perfectly and they could now see what Hugh from C.A.S.I. was talking about.

The smooth walls were covered with engravings of inscriptions next to drawings that were obviously stars and solar systems. The twins started studying them immediately, whispering excitedly to each other.

In the meantime, Lynn and I noticed a circular indent in the floor and moved in for a closer look. There were the typical pottery shards, old pieces that we surmised were once used as tools with six small glass vials that had some residue still stuck at the bottom of each. Lynn held one up to the light, "I have never seen anything like this before," she said, as she turned it over and over in the light.

I continued to scan the room, '*There has to be more than this*,' I thought. Then, in the corner of my eye, I saw a white object against the wall. I took a small soft brush from my kit, walked over to it and started brushing the dirt away. The more I brushed, the more that came to light. It was a skeleton.

"Lynn!"

She rushed over. "Blimey!"

Lynn also took out a small brush and helped me

with clearing the dirt. It took us an hour before the entire skeleton was revealed. The white of the bones was almost blinding, which is unusual for being buried in a dark, damp dungeon for so long.

"This is strange," Lynn said, "they're in perfect condition. No disintegration whatsoever." She picked up the skull to examine it and the bottom jaw fell to the ground.

"Careful!" I scolded. She gave me the 'I'm sorry' look.

"Lynn, check this out. The chest, the sternum has been shattered."

She glanced at it, "A war wound? I guess there's no guessing how he died with a wound like that. Not in here at least. We'll take them to the lab," she said, still turning the skull over in her hands.

"Carlynn, look!" she suddenly shouted and shoved it in my face.

"Alright already!" I said, "What am I looking at?" I no sooner asked the question when I saw the answer. The skull had another row, or rather half row of teeth behind the first.

VLAD DRACUL

"Carlynn!" Lynn shouted again, while pointing at the chain around the neck; the pendant had an emblem. I picked it up carefully to examine it closer, "Dracul, order of the dragon, Vlad," I read aloud.

Rae and Jade turned, eyes wide, the curator froze, "Is it him?" he asked quietly.

"Yes, it appears to be," Lynn quietly answered.

"Hold on," I cautioned, "We don't know that for sure. We need to examine the skeleton more closely, get a carbon dating … wait," turning the pendant around, "the back has a small marking and check this out!"

Lynn grabbed the pendant from me, "I am Vlad," she whispered, slowly lowering it, "Holy shit! Do you think it's real?"

No one said a word. You could hear a pin drop.

"Ok, ok, before we get carried away, let's collect what we can and do a little more studying," Jade said, bringing us all back down to earth. "Carlynn, Lynn, pack up those bones and whatever else you can get your hands on that we can remove from the site. Rae, get the camera and start taking pictures of the walls. Make sure you get everything. We'll upload them and take a closer look. We may need to contact S.E.T.I. and see if they can help figure out what these star maps mean."

Without another word, we proceeded with Jade's instructions, packing up everything we could. Even the curator helped. Rae was busily snapping pictures.

"You have to secure this site, Mikhael," I ordered.

The curator smiled, "Will do, but I don't think anyone else will find it," he answered.

"Well, if you did then…" I countered.

He sighed, "Yes, you're right. I will have guards watch the castle. We will postpone all tours, indefinitely. The council will not be happy but I will explain the situation."

"Don't 'explain' too much though," Lynn said, "We want to keep this quiet. At least until we know what exactly what we're dealing with."

"Don't worry, the council is versed in the importance of secrecy. They will be completely silent," he said.

"I hope so," I said.

We took everything to Mikael's residence, where he just happened to have a large laboratory attached at the rear of the house.

"Wow!" Lynn gasped.

"Convenient," I observed.

Mikael explained, "This is my own personal laboratory, however, I was able to call in a few favours and gathered every piece of equipment I thought you may need."

"Nice," Rae said.

****

The castle had that eerie glow from the illuminating flood lights. Security was increased by three. Still wasn't enough according to Mikael, but it was all he could get on short notice.

The night was completely black with no moon and only the stars twinkled like tiny strobes.

All was quiet as the time hit 8:30pm and the guards checked in with one another. A problem quickly came to light when two guards did not respond. The three remaining gathered together and set out to search for them. 'Probably just messing around,' one guard thought. They made their way around what was thought to be the rear entrance of the castle. "Look at that idiot, sleeping on the job," one said. "I will be reporting this to the curator!" As they approached him, they shone the flashlight in his face and quickly saw that he wasn't asleep. He was dead.

His skin was white as fresh fallen snow, his eyes

permanently wide open and his facial expression was that of surprise.

Suddenly a scream tore through the night from just meters away. They ran towards the sound to find a second guard on the ground, with a figure hovering over him.

"Hey!" one guard yelled. The figure turned, saw the guards and quickly disappeared. He was so fast they couldn't guess which way he headed. Instead they went to their fallen comrade's aide. He was still alive, although barely.

"I cannot move, I cannot move," he kept repeating, weakly.

"Oscar, look at me. Did you see who it was?" he asked.

With wide, wild eyes, he said, "Vlad Tepes," over and over, his voice escalating to a scream.

13

POSSIBILITIES

The hotel room sure wasn't like Paris, but it was comfortable. It was large enough, with very plain décor, a tiny bathroom and two queen size beds, which we had to share and that wasn't going to be easy. Four women sharing one small bathroom; let's just say we had to work out a schedule.

There was a knock at the door. Rae opened it and let in Mikhael. By his expression, we knew bad news was coming.

"Ladies, there was an incident at the castle last night," he opened. "One of the guards was found dead and another has been paralyzed."

"Oh my god! What happened?" I asked.

"I cannot say for certain, but the others said that Oscar, the one who is paralyzed, claimed it was Vlad Tepes," Mikael answered.

"Oh come on!" Lynn said, "Now we're supposed to believe that a vampire is on the loose? Really?"

"Um, Lynn, remember the skeleton we found? That second row of teeth sure looked like fangs to me. Am I the only one who saw that?" I asked. Silence surrounded us for about thirty seconds.

"The skeleton we found has already been carbon dated Carlynn. It's at least six thousand years old. Vlad the Impaler lived in the fifteenth century so it can't be him," Lynn said.

"That's not entirely true, Lynn," Jade chimed in, "Rae and I have studied the symbols extensively and we also confirmed with S.E.T.I., who in turn confirmed with NASA and the scientists running the Hubble. Those are star maps. Solar systems and galaxies."

"Yeah," Rae interrupted, "why would those symbols and star maps be in Dracula's castle? We've got to find out what the connection is between the skeleton and that", Rae pointed at the wall, "It doesn't make sense. My instincts tell me they have something in common, but what?"

"There's one more thing. They found a wormhole," Jade said.

"A what?" I asked, not sure of what I heard.

"A wormhole," Jade repeated.

"What does that mean?" I questioned.

"We're not sure, exactly," Rae answered. The twins gave each other one of their looks. The kind that told me they were not revealing all they knew.

"Ok, I saw that," I accused, "Time to spill, you two."

Rae and Jade whispered to each other, quiet enough that neither of us could hear and finally Rae said, "Tell them!"

Jade sighed and said, "There's one thing we suspect.

We need to consider what Rae and I and many others think; that we are not alone." Rae continued, "Carlynn, you and Lynn have degrees in ancient history. Have you ever wondered where all the legends come from? The gods, the monsters, demons, vampires, etc., where did it all start? Is it not possible that Earth has been visited before by someone out there?" She pointed upward, "According to the time line of our galaxy, Earth is a very young planet. Others have been around a lot longer and many from other systems may have come here. Maybe even made Earth their home!"

"And this 'wormhole' is some sort of transport system, I'm assuming?" I asked.

The twins stood, looking wide-eyed at Lynn and myself. Mikhael couldn't believe what he was hearing, "Ladies, really. You expect me to believe you? This is preposterous!"

"No, no, wait a sec Mikhael. They have a point. Why else would you hire them to come here? Deep down, you suspected something like this, didn't you?" I grilled.

He bent his head and nodded.

"Alright, Ancient Aliens!" Lynn said, "This will be

fun!"

"Except this is the real thing, Lynn, not a TV show," I said.

Her broad smile didn't change, "And the TV show is not based on reality?"

14

DIGGING DEEPER

The connection to his father the second time was a success, however short the conversation was. At least he got to speak to his mother for a moment.

He recalled the tears in her eyes, both happy and sad. Varian assured her he was doing fine and not to worry. His father, however, had instructions for him instead. Varian was to return to Europe. He had balked at his father's orders, but Valan had been adamant that he follow through. When the connection was lost, Varian immediately set out for Romania. He didn't bother with the airlines this time. He could get there faster on his own. Besides, the only reason he used human means of transport was to fit in to the main stream populous. If humans knew Genesians inhabited their planet, what would they do to them? He was in no mood to find out. This human race needed more time to evolve first.

ROMANIA

Until now, Varian had no idea he could contact his father from this place. He assumed that he had to go back to his original landing spot. 'Why couldn't it have been closer?' he thought, as he trudged up the hill to the castle ruins.

The time was midday and the sun shone brightly. He would have been a little sunburned if it weren't for the sunscreen he used. On his home planet, his people didn't need such a concoction. Their sun was farther away and the atmosphere was protected by an extra ozone layer, or so his father told him. He wasn't sure. He wished he'd listened more closely to his father when he was younger.

The entrance was upon him. He paused for a moment to catch his breath. He would need to feed soon as it had been three days since his last one. He could usually go at least a week before needing food again but he had used a lot of energy climbing mountains in the light of day. '*You can wait a while longer,*' he had convinced himself.

Varian followed his father's instructions and found the dungeon, tapped the brick, opening the door, albeit with an uneasy silence.

He could smell it instantly; humans. They've found this place and he must let his father know as soon as he could.

A noise from outside the stone door forced him to hurry to the dark side of the room. An image of a human woman stepped in the room. Being so close to one renewed his growing hunger and his weapons emerged automatically. 'Stop it!' he scolded himself.

He watched as she knelt down in the center circle and started brushing dirt, carefully. 'What's she doing?' he wondered. He watched her brush, pick up small pieces and put them in bags. This went on for some time and he was getting impatient. So much so, he inadvertently let out an exasperated sigh.

"Hello? Is someone there?" she called out.

He froze, '*dammit*,' he cursed himself.

She took a flashlight and slowly scanned the circular room. Varian moved as the light approached, always avoiding detection, until he had to move more quickly. The oncoming light was pushing him to a section that wasn't completely dark and he would surely be easily spotted. He rushed past her in a blur of speed and she felt the breeze.

"Hey!" she shouted, "who's there?"

She hardly asked the question when she found herself pinned down on the ground, unable to move.

"You!" she gasped.

"You?!!" he reiterated.

15

GENESIA

Genesia is a planet located in the Keplar system 500 light-years from Earth. Scientists on our planet know it as Keplar 186f, thought to be habitable. If they only knew the truth because their theory is right. The difference is, it's already populated by a race that knows about us, but we don't know about them.

Valan and Nemar decided to work together – they had come to this conclusion after Nemar forced her husband to reveal the truth about his recent actions. He had been distant, going out at all hours and using feeble excuses as to where he'd been and what he was doing. Valan didn't want her to worry but Nemar insisted she would feel better about Varian's predicament if she could assist in searching for the truth.

"You will not stop me from helping exonerate Varian!" she yelled; Valan relented.

The two decided to travel to the area of the city where the crime was committed. Perhaps there were witnesses who were overlooked or refused to come forward.

They arrived on the scene where the body was found, the area now completely encased in protective glass. Law keepers hadn't taken it down, which was very odd. Usually, the protective glass was removed the day after sentencing. Varian's sentencing was long over and he was now on Earth, never to return.

"What is this?" Nemar asked

"I don't understand either my love," Valan

answered.

They started going from dwelling to dwelling, asking for information from the residents. No one would talk to them, instead they would slam the door shut.

"Valan, anyone who sees us is scared to death," Nemar observed.

"Agreed, curious. These people are afraid to talk to us and I don't know why, but I intend to find out," Valan said.

They headed back to their craft when they heard, "Pssst!"

Valan looked to his left and saw someone behind a small dwelling, a cloaked figure, waving frantically at them.

The cloaked figure led them down a cleverly hidden passage under the dwelling. Once inside, the figure closed the entrance, and flipped his hood off.

"Kaeton!" Nemar exclaimed.

"Shhhh!" Kaeton cautioned.

"What is this?" Valan demanded.

"Please keep your voice down or someone will hear," Kaeton begged.

He looked haggard, his eyes sunken, complexion pink, a sign he hadn't fed for some time. His hair messed and matted and his clothes, torn and dirty.

"Kaeton, what's happened to you?" Nemar's concern was immediate.

"I've been in hiding, madam Kanor," his voice was shaky.

"Why?" Valan asked.

"Baxor and his father deemed me a threat, sir."

Nemar and Valan gave him an expectant look while Kaeton paced, rubbing his hands, thinking about how he would go about explaining to the Kanors, the parents of one of his best friends, exactly what happened the night of the murder.

"Oh, get on with it man," Valan whispered, harshly. Nemar touched her husband's arm, telling him to keep calm.

"Baxor killed Gengie Daj, not Varian!" he blurted out.

Nemar and Valan stood motionless, in complete shock for a moment. Then Valan spoke, "What happened, Kaeton, tell me."

He began.

"We were walking home that night, talking, laughing, having a good time, when Baxor said he was hungry and Madoc suggested a depot only a couple of blocks away. Baxor spotted Gengie Daj and said, 'I have a better idea,' then he attacked. We stood by watching, not knowing what to do. Varian was the only one who called out for Baxor to stop, but he ignored him. Afterward, Varian tried to convince Baxor to turn himself in but he refused. Instead, he called for his father to pick us up. He threatened all of us; he said he'd kill us, our families, friends and anyone else we were close to. Varian wouldn't back down so Baxor's father called the Voicer and the law keepers, pretending to agree to turn his son in but he lied. When the Voicer arrived, he accused Varian and we backed up the accusation. We were afraid. Terrified, actually."

"Then you should be safe," Nemar said, "Why are you hiding, what changed?"

"I found out more. Much more. What I know makes Varian's sentence a walk in the park. Right now, I consider him the lucky one."

16

CONFRONTATION

Two figures stood silently at opposite sides of the circular room staring at one another.

'*Ok, enough of this*,' I thought, "Varian, why are you here?" I asked.

"I could ask you the same," he answered, rather defiantly.

"Fine, you can leave now before you get in trouble. This is a closed site."

"I'm not the one who will leave, Carlynn. You are," he snapped, "you should not be here. You have no idea what you're dealing with."

"That's what I'm here to find out."

"Ah, yes, the archeologist/anthropologist," he saw the shock in my face, "yes I know what your profession is, but you will find nothing here. Leave!" he demanded.

"No!"

I didn't see it happen, but I found myself pinned against the wall, Varian's face just inches from mine.

"I will not tell you again," he warned. His eyes were almost black and I could swear he bared his teeth at me. I must have been seeing things.

"I don't know what you have to do with any of this but I will not be bullied or threatened. I'm staying right here." I said, calling his bluff. I knew I was risking my safety or even my life, but this was one of those times where I shot my mouth off and only considered the consequences afterward. You could call it courage, bravery or heroic, but this time, it was sheer stupidity. It was obvious Varian was extremely strong, fast and could kill me in an instant. I took one hell of a shot and it worked; he let me go.

Taking a minute to gather my thoughts, I then asked, again, "Who are you, really ... and what are you doing here?"

"I'm Varian Kanor," he answered.

"And..."

"You would not believe me if I told you and it may be risky for you to know."

"I'll decide that, if you don't mind. This 'dig' is getting weirder by the day. First, I'm hired to go on the strangest dig ever, then told we may be investigating the possibility of ETs and I find that skeleton, which is thought to be Vlad; turns out that's not possible."

"Wait, you've found Vlad? Where is he? Was there a pendant around his neck? Where..."

"Slow down, man. We know that it's not him and yes, he had a pendant around his neck. How did you know?"

"It is him. I was sent here to find Vlad and the pendant."

"Ok, what's so special about it?" He didn't answer.

"Look, I can't help unless you give me a little info Varian. You can tell me, you know. Really, I'll keep my mouth shut, I promise," I vowed, hoping I could keep that vow. I pushed a little more, "If I can help you, maybe you can help me."

He continued his silence for what seemed like hours, pacing around the room, glancing at me a few times, no doubt deciding whether I was trustworthy or not. He finally stopped, sighed, "Alright, I don't know what else to do, but you must swear to complete secrecy on what I'm about to tell you," he said.

I nodded. His actions and tone told me this was no joke and if I didn't agree, he could kill me, maybe even go after Lynn, Rae and Jade or even Mikhael. He also knew where I was from and could easily hurt my parents in an act of revenge.

"We'll need some privacy," he said, as he closed the large brick door.

17

FRIENDS

"What if someone walks in on us?" I asked.

"They can't," he replied, "I've locked it."

"Oh."

I didn't know the door could be locked, and neither did anyone else, I surmised. He motioned for me to sit down and that meant on the dirt floor. I sat down; so did he.

"This is not my home planet," Varian began and before I could ask, he continued, "My home is a planet called Genesia. It's located in the Keplar system. If you gaze at the stars at night, I believe you can find it in one of the constellations. Lyra, right?"

I nodded.

"It is twelve hundred light years away from here."

"That's a very long way. May I ask how you got here?"

"On Genesia there is a device called the P.T.P, Penitentiary Transport Portal. It's a type of travel we've used for many years. I've heard some humans refer to it as a wormhole and I see that there was a television show called Stargate. It's a little surprising to me that humans have evolved so much. Anyway, it's the same premise. We can travel planet-to-planet. Your Earth is the closest to ours and we found it suitable. That's why I'm here."

"Suitable for what?"

"I'm assuming you know your history?" he asked.

"Yes."

"In the eighteenth century of your history, Australia

had a very different purpose right?"

"Yes, how do you … "

"I know all of Earth's history," he interrupted, then continued, "We consider Earth a penitentiary and we have used it for millions of years as one."

"Millions, wait, millions? We consider the human race to be approximately four million years old, evolved from tiny mammals to who we are today," I exclaimed, not sure I believed everything Varian was saying.

He noticed the disbelief, "I assure you, I am telling the truth," he said, calmly.

"There's more," I said, "a lot more."

"Yes, but I think I've revealed enough for now."

"May I ask one more question?"

"Yes."

"What are you?"

The expression on his face told me my question came out wrong – not the first time, "Oh god! I'm so sorry!" I quickly apologized, "Sometimes I ask or talk without thinking first." I decided to shut up before I said anything more that would insult him.

He smiled, "It is ok. I know what you meant. Just

caught me off guard; I am Genesian."

"I know that. I'm human, but my planet is called Earth," I said, in an attempt to redeem myself from the previous question.

"My 'race' is Genesian."

"Oh."

"Now I need a favour from you. I need that pendant."

"It's at the lab … along with the skeleton."

"Vlad," he corrected.

"Ok, Vlad," I concurred, "but we don't know if it's really him."

"It's him," he countered.

I was about to protest and explain that it couldn't possibly be Vlad, when I realized, "Wait, exactly how old was Vlad?"

"He was aged, yes," he answered.

"As in possibly six thousand years or so?" another question I couldn't resist asking.

"Yes."

I'm sure my expression was of complete shock, since I was exactly that. Shocked.

"That pendant isn't for esthetics. It's a communication device."

There was a noise from the other side of the door.

"Damn, someone's here," I whispered.

"I have to go."

"But they'll see you."

"You didn't," he quipped, smiled that perfect smile, opened the door and disappeared.

Lynn and the twins entered the room, "Wow, I felt a breeze," Lynn said, "which is unusual, since we're so far down."

18

HE'S BACK

It was midnight and I couldn't sleep. The encounter with Varian, and all the stories he told me; it was difficult to absorb. My imagination was running wild.

I heard a light rap on the door. I sat up in bed and looked over at Lynn, who was out cold. Rae and Jade, ditto.

I hear the rapping again, so I climbed out of bed and went to the door, opened it quietly, and saw Varian.

"What are you doing here?" I whispered, as I shut the door behind me leaving the both of us in the hallway.

"I don't sleep," he replied.

"Uh, ok, Genesians don't sleep?" another question.

"Not here," he whispered, "something about your atmosphere. We don't need it."

I waited.

"I need Vlad's communication device," he said.

"It's in a safe at the lab. I can't just take it," I said.

"You don't have to. I'll retrieve it," he said, "now that I know where it is."

"You can't. Mikhael is sending it away in the morning."

"Where?" he snapped and grabbed my hand.

"Whoa, stop it," I said, pulling my hand away but couldn't. He had a tight grip, "can I have my hand back?"

His face softened and he loosened his hold, but didn't let go completely. Neither did I, I mean, who'd object to a hot guy holding their hand?

"Would you go for a walk with me?" he whispered.

I nodded, "Oh, uh, give me a minute to change."

"Don't have to on my account," he smiled.

I raised my brow, an expression that comes natural to me, "ha, ha," I said, as I opened the door and tiptoed back into the room. I headed for the bureau where my clothes were, discarded my t-shirt, grabbed a pair of jeans, a light sweater, rushed to put my sneakers on, picked up a hoodie and darted out the door. My friends didn't hear a thing, '*whew*'. Thank goodness because I was sure they'd protest my midnight venture, especially with Varian. They've made their feelings clear about him. They don't trust him and are afraid of him. The twins hate him more than anyone else, though I can't get the reason out of them. Very frustrating.

We left the hotel and started walking down the quiet street. It was a nice evening but a little chilly, compelling me to slip on my hoodie. We talked more. He asked me about my life and I obliged, a little. As I talked about my childhood, I wondered why in the world he'd be interested. I even mentioned my first encounter with him and how it freaked me out. It made him laugh, "I was hoping you'd forgotten," he said.

"How could I?"

"You were a lovely little girl, Carlynn."

"Um, thanks?"

"You're wondering."

"Wondering what?" I asked, knowing full well what I wanted to know and so did he, "Why I haven't aged," he answered.

"Yes," I said quickly, but was sure of the answer. One myth about vampires was correct, they don't age. There, I said it, vampire … and they stay young forever.

The idea that vampires really exist is hard to believe but here I am walking and talking with one and I realized, I'm not afraid. Varian didn't exhibit any threat.

"So, Vlad the Impaler was a real vampire," it wasn't a question.

"That's an interesting word, 'vampire.' It sounds so ominous and almost violent; I prefer Genesian."

"You don't age."

"No, not here at least."

"You drink blood."

"Yes."

"That's enough for now; change the subject."

"Ok, we'll change the subject," he agreed, but his smile never faded.

I smiled, he took my hand and we continued our walk. Time got away from us. Before we knew it, dawn was creeping up on us. Varian reached into his coat, pulled out a pair of Serengeti sunglasses and put them on.

"You are sensitive to sunlight," I observed.

"Yes we are. It will not kill me, as your predecessors seem to think, but your sun is closer to Earth and we are not used to it. I would get one hell of a sunburn," he said as he pulled out a bottle of sunblock.

I giggled, "Really, sunblock? What a cliché."

"Yeah, I know," he laughed along, "but you wouldn't want to see me without it, believe me."

He applied the lotion and put the bottle back in his jacket pocket.

"You should go back."

I checked my watch, "I guess so. The girls will be wondering where I am," I said, "Oh wait!"

"That's ok, I will get it myself."

"Oh, just be careful."

19

FACING THE MUSIC

"Where have you been?" Lynn snapped as soon as I walked in the door.

"Out," I replied, rather sheepishly.

"Where?" Rae demanded.

"I think it should be 'with who?'" Jade said.

'*Dammit, they know*,' I thought, "Um, with Varian,"

I answered in a whisper, awaiting the backlash.

"Told you girls," Jade said. All three stood, arms crossed, staring at me with anger and shock in their eyes.

Calling home again…

The device was exactly where Carlynn said it would be. Varian found that breaking into a safe was child's play. The safe was two feet by two feet, with a combination lock. '*This is why Mikhael wants to send its contents away,*' he thought, '*this is not a 'safe' safe at all.*' He broke it open, spotted the triangular shape and grabbed it. Moving so fast, Mikhael felt only the breeze when he opened the door to the lab; Varian simply slipped by unseen.

He made his way back to the castle and down to the dungeon. The room was quiet – no one had been there since he and Carlynn's last meeting was interrupted. Good, he needed to be alone.

He took out his cell phone, the one he altered so he could contact his father, and placed it on one side of the indented circle and placed Vlad's directly opposite. He touched the 'on' button of his cell and watched the lasers from each one meet in the middle. The light expanded, "Father," Varian called out, "are you there?"

"I'm here son," his father answered. He saw his father's face come into view, "I'm coming," Varian said as he took a step toward the center of the beam, "Stop!" Valan shouted. Varian did as he was told and in confusion asked, "Why?"

"The PTP has been sabotaged!" he managed to say before Baxor pushed him from view, "Hey buddy, how's life on your home?"

"Baxor!?! What are you doing? Where's my father?"

"Oh don't worry, my friend. The Voicer has taken your father and mother to a safe place. It is too bad your father couldn't mind his own business really, because he now knows more than he needs to and that makes him a bit of a risk."

"If you hurt them, Baxor, I will kill you!" Varian promised.

Baxor laughed, "You are light years away and your

father was right. You will die if you try to come back right now. See, they found out a little too much in their search for evidence that proves your innocence and Kaeton, tsk tsk, Poor Kaeton. He just couldn't keep quiet. He has paid the price, as has his family," Baxor smiled the perfect evil smile.

"Why have you done this? I don't understand."

"Well, my friend, my little indiscretion was drastic I admit, but I couldn't take the blame because I'm slated for a more important task in the near future and if I was convicted, my future would be ruined, to say the least. Don't worry Varian, I'll be seeing you very soon."

"Baxor!" a voice Varian recognized – the Voicer, "That's enough!" The connection died and Varian stood shocked, dumbfounded, "What the hell is happening?" he whispered.

"Hey, hey," I wanted to ease their worry, "It's ok! Varian is far from dangerous."

"Really? Why is he here? Is he following us, or

more specifically, you?" Lynn questioned. The next question came out of the blue, "He's a vampire, isn't he?" Rae and Jade asked in unison. I couldn't answer.

"Carlynn," Lynn said.

"No, of course not," I replied a little too quickly.

"You're lying," again in unison.

"You two are freaking me out right now."

"Truth, Carlynn," Lynn demanded. I looked each one in the eye and realized I didn't have a choice, "Yes," I squeaked.

"Jade, call down to room service. We're staying in for a breakfast meeting," Rae commanded, "and we'll need to be alone instead of in a crowded restaurant, too public." I excused myself and slipped into the bathroom.

Halfway through breakfast and still no one spoke. I sighed; I'd have to start the discussion, "So, let's have it," I opened.

"Fine," Lynn started, "you know nothing about this guy and spend the entire night with him. He admitted he is a vampire and still you choose to keep company with him. He's dangerous Carlynn."

"If he's so dangerous, I wouldn't be here, Lynn," I

argued, "We talked, and that's all."

"About what?" Rae asked.

"Things."

"Carlynn, what can you tell us about him? You may as well fill us in. The more we know, the easier it will be to protect ourselves," Jade said. Rae glanced at Jade, then nodded. That's when it dawned on me, "Telepathy! Oh my god, you two can communicate through telepathy!" I shouted, excitedly, "How did I miss that? The signs were there and I missed it!"

Lynn's eyes popped, "Really?"

"Shhhhh," Jade hushed, "you can't tell anyone, ever. Some weirdo, psycho scientists tried to make lab rats out of us when we were younger."

"That must have been rough."

"It was, on us and our parents. Jade and I made up our minds that we'd never let anyone know again. I guess we let our guard down."

"Don't be so hard on yourselves. Carlynn's pretty sharp, she knew there was something about you two that wasn't 'normal'. I'm just surprised it took her this long to figure it out."

"Hey!"

The girls laughed, breaking the tension, "Your secret will always be safe with us," I promised. Lynn nodded in agreement.

"Thanks."

It didn't take long before we were back to the real topic: Varian. We ended up in a heated debate, the twins were con, I was pro and Lynn was on the fence.

"You don't know what he's capable of."

"I know some."

"But not all."

"I know enough for now and I also know that I'm not in any danger," I reiterated.

All three sighed, "She's not going to stop seeing him," Lynn said.

"Fine, if you insist on keeping contact with him, will he talk to us?" Jade asked.

"I'll ask him."

20

CANADA BOUND

Back at the lab, Lynn and I were busy taking measurements, piecing together shards, making notes. Jade and Rae were going over the enlarged images of symbols, theorizing their meanings.

"We need to talk to Varian. He could tell us what these mean," I overheard Rae whisper, "I'm tired of guessing."

"Guessing?" Jade responded.

"Shhhhh."

I glanced at Lynn. We knew there was more about the twins we wanted to know, but now was not the time.

"Ladies," Mikhael entered the lab, "Hugh Morgan just called and he wants you back at the institute. You'll be leaving in three hours. Get packed."

"What about our work?" I asked.

"Everything will be packed up properly and sent as soon as possible," he promised.

Why did the trip home seem to take forever?

Hugh met us at the airport with a car waiting and rushed us back to C.A.S.I. He wouldn't say anything in the car except, "We'll talk at the institute."

We were immediately rushed into the boardroom, "What the hell is going on?" I demanded, "Your behaviour is bizarre to say the least."

"Sit," he said; we complied.

"Mikhael is dead."

"What? How? He can't be dead, we just left him ten hours ago," Lynn said.

"He and two of his colleagues were packing the artifacts. The two men took some parcels to the van for transport and when they returned, he was dead. A hole in his chest and everything you found in the castle, gone."

Silence followed.

"There's more. Whoever did it, left a warning note and it read as follows: 'You will cease this investigation immediately or there will be consequences. We are watching you to be sure you will comply with our wishes.'"

"What have we gotten ourselves into," Lynn whispered.

It was safe to say that we were sincerely scared, "We're being watched?" I asked.

"Not here, but when you leave the institute..." he didn't finish.

"What do we do?"

"You go home, all of you. You give the appearance that all is well but I want you to refrain from talking or seeing each other for at least a week," Hugh said.

"Scatter, go our separate ways?" Rae asked.

"For now. We'll be in contact with you periodically,

throughout the week and keep you up-to-date. We want to give the illusion that we've complied with their wishes, whoever they are."

"Want to go home now," Jade said. The sisters rose, took each other's hand and left.

"You two should go, too," Hugh urged.

I wanted to run after Rae and Jade and force them to tell me everything they knew. They were not being truthful about something; I could feel it.

"Carlynn."

"Yes."

"Let's go."

"I'm coming."

We left the building, said our good-byes, promising to keep in touch via text, and parted ways. I decided to head back to the country, to my parents. Home.

It had only been three weeks since I was last there, but it felt like three years. I felt like a stranger in my own home. My parents immediately noticed a change in me, "Are you alright, Carlynn?" my mother asked, the consummate worry wart. "I'm fine mom."

"Can you tell me what happened in Romania? I

know something did. You're different and that worries me."

"I'm ok mom, and no, I'm sorry, I can't tell you anything right now."

"Ok. When you're ready, I'll be here."

"Thanks. I'm going for a walk."

"Be careful."

"Always am."

Duke was by my side as usual. We walked along the fence line checking for breaks in the barbed wire or a broken post. A habit I picked up from my dad. He would check the fence once a week. I came to think he'd use the time for himself also. A peaceful walk alone to gather his thoughts.

I didn't realize I was back at the hole in the ground; the star landing. I sat at the edge again and thought about recent events.

"So you are back."

The voice made me jolt and he stepped from behind a large tree. Varian.

"Are you following me? What the hell!"

"No."

"Then what are you doing here?"

"I had to."

"Why?"

"It's a long story."

"As it turns out, I have time."

21

VARIAN'S STORY

Varian walked around the small clearing and came across the large tree he had downed, "Did you do that?" I asked.

"Yes."

"Wow, I assume you were angry at the time?"

"Somewhat."

"If this is what you are capable of when you're just a little angry, I'd hate to see what you'd do when you're furious."

He laughed, "I hope you never have to see that."

There were a few seconds of silence, then I had to ask, "You arrived here through the PTP right?"

He nodded.

"So, this is your prison?"

"Yes."

"What did you do on Genesia to warrant this kind of prison sentence?"

"I'm convicted of a murder I didn't commit."

"Oh my god, they were right, you are dangerous."

"Who said I was dangerous?"

"Lynn, Rae and Jade, my friends."

"They're wrong."

"They've figured you out; they know you're a vampire."

"Genesian."

"Semantics."

"Not to me. Carlynn, I'm not dangerous, I was wrongly convicted and I've been communicating with my father back home. He's been working hard to find the evidence that will exonerate me. After our evening together, I went back to the castle and made contact with him, but he had company. The Voicer and Baxor, they caught him. We who are convicted are forbidden to have any contact with our families."

"Ever?"

"Never. Baxor, he was the one who committed the murder and I tried to stop him. He accused me and had my friends Jez, Kaeton, and Madoc back up his lies. They've taken my parents; I'm afraid of what they'll do to them. The last thing Baxor said to me was 'see you soon'.

"Can't you go back through the portal?"

"I was going to do just that when my father stopped me. Apparently, the Voicer and Baxor sabotaged the device. If I had gone through, it would have killed me."

"What will you do?"

"I don't know yet. I have no friends here, no contacts…"

"You have me."

He smiled, sat down beside me, and took my hand, "Thanks. To be honest, you are the first human I've befriended."

"Really? You've never bothered to blend in with us?"

"No. I was afraid to be discovered, as your friends have now done."

"I'm afraid that's my fault. They came to the only conclusion they could after finding Vlad, the necklace bearing his name and the fangs."

"Ah yes, those are a necessity. I trust they will keep my secret? If word is spread that we exist and live here on Earth, there could be widespread panic."

I wondered how this being came to our planet, was condemned to live with us forever and yet knows nothing about us. Especially when it came to so-called mythical figures of our history, "Believe me, even if we said anything, we'd be laughed at. Humans consider you a myth, or at least most do. There are some who believe you exist, but they are considered fanatics."

"Those few are the ones I have to be wary of?"

I knew it was probably a stupid question, but I had to know, "Do you eat human food?"

"No, I get sick."

"Garlic?"

He laughed, "Myth."

"Stake through the heart?"

"Not possible. Our skeletal structure is hundreds of times stronger than that of humans. You can't break through, unless of course, you would use one of those missiles your armies love to use and I'm not willing to test that theory."

"Are you vulnerable to anything?"

"I am weaker during the day, stronger at night and you already know about the sunblock I use."

"Yeah," I giggled.

"The only vulnerability is another Genesian, either by draining the fluids or busting through the breast bone. Genesians are the only ones strong enough to do it."

I winced.

"Sorry."

"It's fine. I did ask."

"You should know we were much like humans many years ago. Evolution made us what we are today."

"So this could happen to us? We could evolve into 'vampires', for lack of a better word?"

"I don't know, but the human race is young and still growing."

"Incredible."

"Why aren't you afraid of me?" he asked.

"I don't know. You don't scare me at all," I answered.

"You know I can kill you."

"Yes, but I think if you wanted to kill me, you'd have done it already."

He smiled at me and I noticed his skin was different, not a pale porcelain, but a pink hue, "Are you ok?"

He stood up, walked a few feet from me, "It's been a while."

"'A while', what? Oh, um I'll leave now."

"May I see you again?"

I felt that butterfly leap in my chest, "Yeah, you know where I'm staying this week. My parents are…"

"I know where they live," he smiled again but this time the perfect pearly whites had sharp canine; I still had no fear.

THE HUNGER

Varian cursed himself for revealing his weapons to her, something he never wanted her to see. His hunger was getting to him and they came out automatically. This time, a filthy woodland creature wouldn't do, he needed more; he needed human blood.

Within minutes, he was in Winnipeg, the closest city

with a larger population, which meant an array of humans out on the streets. More specifically, the homeless. Dusk was upon the city and soon the night would come.

It's not as though the homeless were deserving of the fate he was about to inflict but they were easier prey and he always made sure he found the poor soul who was already dying. He tried to justify that he was giving the ailing human, who had no hope, a peaceful ending. Ensuring he or she felt no pain, an end to their suffering. He would do his best to make certain Carlynn never found out he fed on humans occasionally. She would not understand.

They used to do the same on his home planet; prey on each other. As the animal population dwindled, Genesians evolved, ending up with a new weapon, long canine fangs. For some time, they drank from their prey, ensuring not to kill them. Just take what they needed, but they discovered there was a deadly consequence. If the animal didn't die, they became sick, diseased and the disease spread amongst the nearby animals also, killing them within four days.

So evolution had its drawbacks and in desperation,

the Genesians turned on one another. The result being a fast dwindling population.

The world government had to step in, enforce martial law and develop a blood substitute. This arduous task had been a battle, years in the making. They had no choice but to use their own people as guinea pigs for testing the blood substitute. Many died as a result and their massive planet's population shrank to one hundred million. His father told him this dark history of Genesia when he was a child and it frightened him. What if it happened again? What if the food supply ran out and they turned on one another?

The smell of a dying soul caught his senses and he followed it to a dark narrow alleyway. There, curled up in a fetal position, was an elderly woman, barely breathing.

Varian approached, a quick nip on her wrist injected the paralyzing agent throughout her body. He could feel her relax, "you will be at peace now," he whispered in her ear and sank his weapons deep. He felt himself re-energize almost instantly.

Just as he felt her life end, "Well, well, what an interesting turn of events."

Varian dropped the elderly woman, turned with every intention of killing the person who dared sneak up on him, but stopped short.

"Baxor," he couldn't believe his eyes. Was he dreaming, delusional? He shook his head, "it can't be."

"I can assure you, it is," Baxor stepped toward the dirty, ragged body, limp on the ground, "This one was dying anyway wasn't she Varian?" Varian refused to answer.

"Now I know you can talk, friend, you did plenty of it back home. In fact, you tried to have me convicted because of that unimportant Gengie Daj."

"I am not your friend. you killed Gengie and framed me for it; you are no friend."

Baxor shrugged. His indifference infuriated Varian, "What have you done to my parents?" he demanded, "If you have hurt them in any way, your fate is certain."

"They are in a safe place."

"I should kill you now. At least my sentence would be deserving."

"But you won't because, if the Voicer doesn't hear from me, he has his orders," Baxor responded, "Hear me out Varian. I have a good reason for my actions."

DESPERATE MEASURES

"If this isn't the grandest of explanations, I will make you feel pain, Baxor," Varian threatened.

"I promise it is. Let's walk, I just got here so I haven't had a chance to do any sightseeing."

They walked along the dark streets for a few minutes in silence when Baxor cleared his throat, "Here it goes," he began, "Genesia is dying, Varian. Our resources are running out and our home has, at best, one hundred Genesian years left."

"Our planet is dying is what you're saying"

"No, not the planet per se; our resources. The products used to develop the plasma substitute is running out and we can't duplicate it synthetically. Our scientists have been trying for many years and have failed at every attempt. We have to move the population to a new planet if we want to survive and Earth is the closest with virtually the same atmosphere and eco-system. This planet has approximately seven billion inhabitants, more than enough to sustain us until we find the plant source from which we can develop a new plasma substitute. Now that we know what to look for, our transition should be a smoother one. Only the highest in our government know the truth, Varian, including my father."

"Our brilliant scientists couldn't prepare for this? It's a plant! What the hell. They couldn't do a little gardening? They..."

"Varian," Baxor interrupted, "they did exactly that, but a virus has attacked it and our cure only works on the few that are stronger than the rest. The result was smaller crops and before you ask, no, we can't kill the virus. Not for lack of trying though."

"When is this migration to Earth going to begin?" Varian asked.

"Soon, but there's a catch; only half of Genesians will be allowed to come. The rest must stay behind."

"And die."

"Yes. Earth is too small to accommodate all of us and Varian, you and your parents weren't chosen to make the journey."

"Why not?"

"I don't know. When I found out none of my friends were chosen, I had to find a way. That's why I did what I did."

"Gengie Daj."

"Yes. Jez, Kaeton, and Madoc. I had to think of a way for them also. When Kaeton overheard me and my father discussing it, my father wanted him killed. If what is coming gets out to the public, there will be total anarchy. We have to keep this quiet," Baxor explained.

"What happened to Kaeton? I know he was with my

parents when they were captured."

"I managed to send him through the PTP, he and his family."

"How?"

"It wasn't easy. I'll spare you the details, but rest assured they are here, on Earth, somewhere."

"What about my parents, Jez and Madoc?"

"I'm still working on that. My visit here is a short one. I'm scheduled to return tomorrow night."

"Won't the return kill you? When I tried to get back, you said it would kill me."

"The Voicer did adjust the PTP at my request, but it's fine now. I couldn't let you come back. Do you understand, Varian? This is your home now and soon the home of Genesians," Baxor said.

Varian remained quiet as the two strolled along, his mind racing in an attempt to absorb Baxor's story. It was hard to believe, Genesia, his home, gone for good. No hope of ever returning and Earth was now home. It was incredible and frightening at the same time. He thought of Carlynn. Should he tell her and if he did, could she keep the secret? 'She can,' he decided quickly; he found himself wanting to see her, to tell her…now.

"I have to go," Varian said.

"Where?"

"I just have to go. I'll see you when you return and Baxor, I will be expecting to see my family soon, right?" Varian's question had a tone of warning.

"I promise."

Varian nodded and disappeared.

Baxor smiled, his weapons exposed, "Varian, Varian, I'm betting there's a human you've developed a friendship with," he whispered, "so unwise."

He spotted three teens in a back alley, "Hmmmm, prey. Think I'll sample the local cuisine."

24

I have to admit I was worried about Varian. He seemed so lost and desperate to get back to his own planet. His own planet...seemed so surreal. He was a real live alien. All myths throughout history of where vampires come from, what their weaknesses are. How they 'spawn from the devil', all wrong. They are simply a different race from another planet. I sat in my room at home, my parent's asleep downstairs. They kept my room the same. It hadn't changed since the day I left for university. I couldn't sleep. Too many things to process and convince myself that this was not all a dream.

"Still awake, I see."

I jumped, "Jesus Varian, you scared the hell out of me," I whispered harshly, "You've got to give me some warning that you're coming!"

"Sorry."

"Shhhh, not so loud."

"Ok," he whispered.

I relaxed and sat back down on the bed, "What brings you back? Did you eat? How are you feeling?"

"I'm fine, thank you," he hesitated, "I ran into Baxor."

"What!?"

"Relax, it's not what it seems. We talked and he told me the truth."

"Tell me."

Varian repeated Baxor's story to me and after he was finished I was dumbfounded.

"Carlynn?"

"Yes."

"You alright?"

"Um, yeah…I think so."

"You sure? You don't look it."

"I'm ok Varian. Wait, that means fifty million Genesians will be coming here. Earth is on the brink of over-population as it is. Where will they all go? How will we feed them and does Earth have the resources to develop the plasma substitute they need?" My questions were flying faster than he could answer; he didn't know all the answers, I surmised.

"Varian."

"Um, I just realized, how could I not think of this sooner? Humans…you will be the Genesian's food until the substitute is ready," he confessed.

"You can't do that!"

Varian took me in his arms and we disappeared from my room. He was so fast, before I knew it, we were back at my star landing site.

"We can talk here. Your parents won't be disturbed."

"How many of us will die?"

"I don't know."

"You have to stop this invasion."

"How?"

"There must be other worlds out there that Genesians can go to."

"There are."

"Why not use one of them?"

Varian was silent, 'Why couldn't they use a different planet?' There were many with similar characteristics and eco-systems to Earth, then he realized, "Oh no," he whispered.

"What?"

"Carlynn, Earth is the only planet because humans are the closest to Genesians. Your species and ours are so similar. We have evolved because we've been around longer."

I found his comment contradictory, "Evolved. Interesting. You said that there is virtually no crime left on Genesia. That you've 'evolved' into a better race. To me, it sounds like your race is reverting back to your roots, Varian."

"You may be right," he responded, sadly.

"I'm terrified; I can't let this happen."

He wrapped me in a warm embrace, I felt so safe with him, "I won't let anything happen to you or your family," he said.

"Promise?"

"Promise."

For a moment I felt like a child again, asking my parents to commit to their promises. We stood in each other's arms for a long time, then he kissed me and that was it. I was a goner!

I didn't want it to end, but a thought occurred, 'What about Lynn, Rae and Jade?' I broke our embrace, "Varian, my friends."

"I will do all I can to keep them safe," he whispered.

I nodded.

"Maybe we should be getting you back. The sun will be up soon and your parents may find you gone."

I no sooner agreed and I was back in my room. "I'll see you soon," he said and disappeared before I could ask when.

It seemed like I'd just fallen asleep when mom was at my bedside shaking me, "Carlynn, sweetheart, time to get up."

"Ah mom, 5 more minutes please."

"What are you, 10?" she laughed and left the room. I sat up, rubbed my eyes, yawned and tried to clear my head. Coffee, I need coffee.

After a quick clean up, I headed to the kitchen straight for the coffee pot. Mom had made a fresh pot and it smelled so good. A dash of my favorite hazelnut flavored cream and I sat down at the table, one last yawn.

A quick glance at the clock on the wall, "Shit, is that the time? I was supposed to text Lynn this morning." Off to my room to fetch my cell and check for messages; eight texts from Lynn:

9:01 am "Hey Carlynn, you up?"

9:06am "Need to talk. Strange guy came to see me last night."

9:30am "He's back."

At 9:32am I missed a call from her, 'Shit!'

9:35am "Told him to leave."

9:36am "Won't go."

9:36am "Need help."

9:45am "Hiding in closet-called 911."

The last one sent me into a panic,

9:46am "Car."

I called her cell, no answer. There was no time to waste. I threw some clothes on, grabbed my bag and ran for the door.

"Where are you off to in such a rush?" mom called out.

"Gotta go mom, work stuff, I'll call you."

"Ok, love you," she called out.

I jumped in my car and sped off the yard. Had to get back to the city. Thankfully Lynn lived in St Boniface, an area easier to get to without having to go through the city or around the perimeter.

I parked, ran for her condo and knocked on the door. Nothing. I banged on the door and pressed the doorbell incessantly.

"Can I help?"

I screamed. Varian was right behind me, "Its Lynn, something's wrong," was all I could get out.

He grabbed my hand and pulled me aside. He faced the door and smashed it open with one hand. "Stay here. I'll check it first." I nodded quickly. It was only seconds and Varian returned.

"Carlynn, she's in bed."

"Ok, ok," I ran in straight for her bedroom.

"Stop," Varian grabbed my arm and held me back.

"Why? Let go!"

"She's asleep, let her rest."

"Nice try, you're a very bad liar. What's wrong?"

"Carlynn," he said, "she's comatose."

"What the hell!" I broke from his grip and ran into the room, "Lynn...Lynn wake up, I'm here."

"She can't, Carlynn."

25

LYNN

He peeked through the bedroom window, care as not to be seen, 'Foolish humans,' Baxor thought as he left the condo. He had a mission to complete. Find the other two. He knew about all four of the women Varian befriended. He'd been watching since the beginning of his sentence. This Rae and Jade, they were special and he intended to find out exactly how special they were. He had his theories but he needed proof. Were they a product of Earth's evolution? It could be. Genesians evolved into who they were at present; why not humans?

There was the possibility, however small, that they were a product of procreation, Genesian and human. The thought made him shudder, '*Disgusting.*' Besides, he'd always been taught Genesians could not procreate with any other species. It wasn't possible.

He realized he'd have to be more convincing to Varian. Show him that communing with humans was not recommended. There would be no future in it. Humans were food.

****

Varian looked out the window and though he saw no one, he knew a Genesian was near, '*He must have left,*' he thought. Then he turned his attention back to the figure, lying motionless in the bed.

I was shaking Lynn, "Please, Lynn, wake up."

"Carlynn, you can't wake her."

"Tell me what happened to her," I demanded.

"Look," he said turning Lynn's head to the side to reveal two small puncture marks on her neck, "She's been attacked."

"By a Genesian."

"Yes."

"Will she be a vam..."

"A vampire?" he interrupted.

I nodded.

"No, not unless the process is completed and..."

"And what?"

"The one who did this has to finish or she will die."

"Die! No!" tears were trickling down my cheeks, "She can't die Varian. How long does she have?"

"Two days at most."

"Wait, you said 'finish'. What did you mean?"

"I mean either she is drained of all blood and dies or she becomes one of us; joined, we call it."

"Then you can do it."

"No, I can't. It has to be the one who started it."

"This can't happen. I won't let her die. Who would do this? How do we find out?"

Varian leaned in close to Lynn and abruptly pulled away. "What is it?" I questioned.

"I know who did this, but I can't believe it."

"Varian, who?"

"Kaeton."

"And he is."

"He's one of my best friends from home," he answered, "Baxor said he'd taken care of Kaeton and his family, that they were here, but had no idea he would be in this city."

"How do you know it's him?"

"Pheromone emittance. We all have a distinct scent. I believe humans have the same."

"Yes, but we can't identify one another."

"We can. Not to say I know every Genesian but I do know the scents of my friends and family and I can detect whether they are Genesian or not."

"Varian, find him please. I can't let her die," I begged. He touched my cheek, "If she is important to you, she is important to me. I will find him."

He vanished.

I wasn't about to leave Lynn's side. All this

happened because I brought Varian into our lives; I was responsible.

A NEW LIFE

Varian scoured the city for Kaeton, '*When I find him, I'll kick his ass first, then drag him back to finish what he started,*' he thought.

Then, on St. Matthews Street, he spotted a hooded figure, lurking behind one of the rooming houses. In a flash he was behind the figure, grabbed the scruff of the neck and slammed him against the house, leaving a dent in the siding, "Ahh!"

"You picked the wrong human," Varian stated.

"Varian! It's great to see you."

"I wish I could say the same, Kaeton."

"Why? You're the first I've seen since I got here."

"I don't think so. You've seen Baxor, haven't you?"

Kaeton hesitated.

"Answer me!" Varian roared.

"How did you know?"

"I know because I've seen him too and he told me everything."

"Oh, so why the attack?"

"Because you went after a friend of mine and left her undone."

"I had to. Baxor ordered me to do it, he didn't give me a choice."

"I don't care. You will come with me and you will finish what you've started," Varian threatened, his weapons bared.

"Whoa, ok, ok, I'm coming. Baxor's gone back home so he won't know anyway."

****

I was holding Lynn's hand. I went through the events of the past few weeks and how I refused to stay away from Varian. If I had listened to her, Rae and Jade, she wouldn't be in this situation. We would've left Romania, not knowing that vampires were real. They'd still be a myth in our eyes and bottom line, we'd be blissfully ignorant of the truth. I longed for ignorance right now.

"Ahem."

I turned to see Varian and a person I assumed was Kaeton. Letting go of Lynn's hand, I rose and attacked him, "Bastard," I screamed while punching and kicking with all my strength. Not that it did any good because it hurt me more than it hurt him. He grabbed my hands, "She's feisty Varian," he said laughing.

"Kaeton, don't," Varian warned, then demanded, "Do this".

He let me go and I ran to Varian, who wrapped his arms around me. It felt safe, felt right. I buried my face in his chest. The tears flowed quickly.

"Sorry," Kaeton apologized, then asked, "are you sure you want me to do this?"

"She can't die," I whispered through my tears.

"But she will be joined, she'll be like us..."

"Please," I begged.

Kaeton looked at Varian, who nodded his consent. He approached Lynn, gently lifted her and found his mark. I watched. I couldn't help it. I watched Lynn's already pale complexion turn to the colour of porcelain.

Kaeton laid her back on the pillow and we waited, "when will she wake up?" I asked.

"Soon," Varian answered.

Lynn stirred. "Lynn!" I broke away from Varian and jumped on the bed next to her.

"Carlynn?" she answered, "That you?"

"Yeah, yeah," I hugged her tight, "you're back, you're back!"

Lynn moaned, rubbed her eyes and sat up, "What the hell happened?" she asked, still groggy, her voice a little raspy.

"You were attacked, Lynn."

"I know that voice," she said, looked up, saw Varian and the stranger who wouldn't leave her alone earlier, "You," she hissed, leaping from the bed so fast, all I saw were flying blankets.

"Lynn don't," Varian shouted.

She had both hands around Kaeton's neck and Varian struggling to pull them away.

"Wow, she's pissed," Kaeton said as he rubbed his neck, Varian still holding her back.

"Lynn," I said, "calm down."

She stopped struggling and Varian felt her relax enough, he felt confident he could release his hold.

"Carlynn," she smiled a perfect white, albeit fanged smile, "where the hell were you? Never mind...my throat hurts...feels dry...bloody thirsty. Carlynn, would you get me some water please?" I looked at Varian who shook his head slightly, 'No.'

"That won't help you, Lynn," Kaeton spoke, "You need something more substantial...and I assure you the taste is much better than water."

"What's going on? Why do I feel...weird?"

Varian sat her down and explained everything to

her. She listened intently and when he was done, she turned to me, "You let them do this? Why?"

"I couldn't let you die," I answered as the tears welled and found the trail down my cheeks once again, "I can't live without my best friend."

"So I'm condemned to being a blood thirst..."

"Hey, watch it," Kaeton interrupted, "Genesian is what we are."

"Sorry," she apologized.

"Kaeton, take her out to feed. You are responsible for her now, you'll have to teach her," Varian said.

"Yeah, ok. We'll leave right now," he answered.

"Wait, wait, why do I have to go?" Lynn asked.

"If Baxor comes back and finds you alive – sorry joined – he will kill you," Kaeton answered, "You were supposed to die, Lynn. Carlynn and Varian made sure it wouldn't happen. Now my family, including myself, are in danger. We have to leave the city. If Baxor finds out what I did, he will...well, you know."

"Yeah," Lynn looked at me, the pain in her eye made me cry again. We hugged tightly, "I will see you again," I sobbed.

"I'm counting on it. You make sure Varian keeps you safe," she whispered. We hugged a little longer. We both knew it would be a long time before we could talk again.

Varian touched my shoulder, "Carlynn," I let go of Lynn.

"I promise to take care of her," he said to Lynn.

"You better! She's in love with you," Lynn exclaimed.

Varian looked directly into her eyes, "You learn fast."

"I'm a genius. Of course I do," she rolled her eyes.

He nodded.

A breeze was felt, then Varian and I were alone.

"You think he believed you?"

"Hook, line and sinker."

The Voicer raised his brows.

"Human expression," Baxor explained, "of course he believed me."

"And if he finds out it's all a fabrication?"

"He won't. We've been best friends since childhood and I know him. He has always trusted my word. He will be with us, you'll see."

"But you have betrayed him already."

"And I have given him an explanation he believed," Baxor snapped, "Don't worry."

The Voicer backed down, but he was worried. If Varian ever found out Baxor lied to him, the whole plan would fall apart, "Your father wishes to see you."

"Now? I just got back."

"His orders were that you see him as soon as you returned."

Baxor let out a loud, exaggerated sigh, "Fine."

The Voicer waited until he was alone, then approached the PTP com. A quick swipe on the screen and the portal was inoperable from the other side.

"What now?" I snapped. I couldn't help it; I was exhausted by the whole Lynn ordeal.

"We need to disappear for a while," Varian said.

"Where?"

"I know a place."

"I can't just disappear...my parents."

"Call them. Tell them, oh I don't know, tell them the institute is sending you on another dig. Or maybe, you're going away with Lynn for a while, tell them anything," I could hear the edge in his voice.

I did call and told them that Lynn and I were off to Egypt on another dig for the institute and that we had to leave immediately. Thankfully, they were supportive and wished me well, mom insisting I call when I had the chance. I played the part well enough that feelings of guilt were rising about lying to them, but they couldn't know the truth. They wouldn't believe it and I wouldn't put them in any danger if I could help it.

Varian took me to a secluded cabin in the woods. More specifically, Riding Mountain National Park.

I had to ask, "Are you allowed to build a cabin here?"

"Didn't ask, just did it."

I didn't bother with explaining that building a cabin in a National Park was illegal as hell. But it was very well hidden and I was pretty sure no one would find it.

We spent our days hiking, talking, and taking in the

scenery and occasionally being whisked up the side of the mountain or one of the taller pines, when Varian saw other hikers coming too close.

The meals consisted of a lot of fast food he'd pick up for me. At least he had the foresight to get salads and wraps instead of burgers and fries. I have to admit, I was self-conscious at first, sitting at the small dining table with him and being the only one eating. When I asked if he was hungry, he'd say he fed already and, "I'm fine."

"Ok."

I slept in the only small bedroom. The double bed was comfortable enough, but there were nights I'd lie awake, my thoughts consumed with the fate of the world, my home. Never mind the unrest between countries, the high risk of global warming and so many social injustices. Human kind has no idea what's coming in the near future. Genesians are far superior in evolution and technology. They've mastered space travel, global peace and solved their food shortage problem. Till now. Tonight was one of those nights again, lying awake wondering about my fate. Varian told me so much about his planet, it seemed as if I'd already been there.

Varian, thinking of him always made my heart beat faster. How is it that a guy who had all the looks could be so loving, caring and considerate? Most guys…argh, I put the thought out of my head, but Varian, he was perfect. Almost too perfect. Then I had a thought, '*What about me? Would he let me die? No, he wouldn't,*' I tried to convince myself. It didn't work. Leaping out of bed, I ran into the living room to see him sitting on a large leather easy chair by a flickering fire, reading. He looked up at me and smiled, "Hey, can't sleep?"

I hesitated.

"Something wrong?"

"What about me?" I blurted out.

"I'm sorry, I don't understand," he said as he got up and stepped toward me.

"Are you going to let them kill me? When Genesians start arriving, will you protect me?"

"Of course I will."

"Really. How? How many are coming? Millions, Varian, millions?"

He wrapped his arms around me, "I won't let anything happen to you, Carlynn."

"What if…?"

"What?"

"…if I was like you?"

"No."

"Why not?"

"Carlynn, by the time Genesians populate this planet, your life span will be over. You'll be able to live out your life, a long and happy one."

Hearing those words, I froze, "Wait. You…me, I thought we had something," I pulled away, "Don't we?"

"Yes, we do."

"But you'd let me grow old and die. Why?"

"Carlynn, we are two different races. Yours is still evolving and who knows what will become of humans. You'd be denied the chance of getting married, having a family…"

"A family that could be – NO – will be slaughtered. Food for Genesians."

Varian stared at me for a long while. In the past, it would have made me shift, turn away uncomfortably. But not now. His eyes were blacker than I'd ever seen. He was angry.

"You did it for Lynn," I whispered.

"For you," he replied, "I need a moment," he left the cabin, leaving the door swinging in the breeze.

28

Varian made his way around the park in minutes, leaving the odd uprooted pine or boulder virtually disintegrated. His anger subsided by the time he returned to the cabin. He admitted Carlynn was right. What kind of life would her children or grandchildren have, if any? Baxor did say the human race would be harvested until they found the resources needed for the substitute.

Something deep down told him Baxor was not

telling the whole story. And then there was Lynn. Would there be any adverse effects of the joining? This was the first time he'd witnessed the joining of a human. He had promised Carlynn that Lynn would be fine, but in truth, he had no idea. He could only rely on Kaeton to keep in contact and inform him of her progress.

"You alright?"

He jumped. No one had ever been able to sneak up on him. He was so lost in his own thoughts that he didn't notice Carlynn behind him. He managed a half-hearted smile, "Yes, I'm ok."

"I'm sorry. I put a lot of pressure on you."

"There's something I haven't told you."

"Yes?"

"To be honest, I have no idea how joining a human will work out in the end."

"Um…you're scaring me. You told me Lynn would be ok and now you say you don't know?"

"We evolved to who we are. We have no idea if humans are strong enough to handle the transition. Your evolution is millions of years behind ours."

"Compatibility factor."

"Right. The only thing I can assure you is Kaeton promised to keep me informed of Lynn's progress."

"Then you must promise to keep me informed also. Varian…promise me."

Varian put his arm around the woman now sitting beside him, "I promise."

We resumed our 'vacation' as best we could. I accepted Varian's decision not to 'join' me, at least for the time being. Although I admit, if he'd chosen to do so, it was a chance I was willing to take.

We spent that evening sitting on the large, soft rug in front of the fire. I giggled inside, thinking what a cliché the rug was. I would have laughed out loud had it been a bear skin rug.

I grabbed a book from a large bookshelf and read aloud. He listened intently, smiling the entire time. I knew he could probably read the book in seconds, but he seemed to enjoy my narration.

"Humans have such imagination," he quipped.

"You acquired this little library," I pointed out.

"Yes, you're right. I enjoy different genres and decided to buy the most popular ones at the time."

"Bram Stoker's Dracula, is an oldie by our standards."

"The very first one I read. Very informative."

I got up and headed for the bookcase, "Let's see, Patterson, Meyer, Claire, Brown, all top sellers, and of course this," I held up the one I was reading, "Harry Potter, JK Rowling, really? Isn't this a children's series?" I laughed.

"Agreed, however, I found I quite enjoyed the story. From what I've discovered, many human adults feel the same," he raised his brow in an accusing expression.

"Ok, I admit, I loved it." We both laughed.

"So, if you've read these already, why am I reading to you?"

"I like the sound of your voice. You have a real passion, something I'm not sure you know you have."

My cheeks felt warm.

"Blushing," he said, "an endearing human quality." He took my hand, led me back to the fire and kissed me softly. I didn't want it to stop at just a kiss. Neither did he.

DINE AND DASH

Kaeton watched Lynn as she made quick use of the armed robber she caught in a dark alley. He'd just shot a clerk at the corner convenience store and ran off with the few dollars in the till. She let the crook drop to the ground when she finished, "Karma is a bitch," she said to the lifeless body.

"Now, now. He may have got what he deserved, but you must appreciate what he has given you," he pointed out.

Lynn smiled, "Ok, you're right."

"Um, you may want to put those away now, "he advised, pointing at her weapons, "We don't want to attract attention."

"Oh."

He watched as Lynn slowly retracted her weapons and the first set moved into place.

"Better?" she smiled.

"Better."

"I don't like doing it, it hurts," she complained.

"Give it time, Lynn. You're like a teething child. The pain will stop soon enough and you'll be able to draw them in a flash. How do you feel?"

"I feel great! Never better!"

"Good, I'll let Varian know of your progress."

A faint ring came from the cell in Varian's pocket.

He took it out, "It's Kaeton. Hey, how's Lynn doing?" He listened closely to Kaeton's report, which seemed to go on for an hour.

"I want to talk to her!" I interrupted; he handed me the cell.

"Lynn?"

"Yeah, it's me."

"How are you? I miss you so much!"

"I'm great, Carlynn. Kaeton's taking very good care of me, don't worry. I gotta run. I'll see you soon."

"When?"

"Soon," she reassured, "Cheers!" and she hung up. I handed the phone to Varian, "What did Kaeton say?"

"Lynn is doing well, but there is one thing that is different."

"What?"

"She can't tolerate sunlight."

"What about the sunscreen? It works for you."

"Carlynn, humans are different, remember?"

"Will it kill her?" my worry rushed back.

"It could. We're not sure. Kaeton said she started burning in the sunlight yesterday. He rushed her to the shadows of the alley and she recovered."

I sighed with relief, "Kaeton better be careful, I might start to like the guy."

Varian raised an eyebrow, "Really?"

I laughed and threw my arms around his neck, "Not in the same way I feel about you," I whispered in his ear. He hugged me tightly.

A large figure behind Varian grabbed his collar, pulling him away from me, "This is a human, Varian!" he roared, "This is food, not anything but food!"

He raised his fist, about to hit Varian and I did the only thing I could think of. With all my strength, my boot made a solid connection between the massive brute's legs. He screamed and fell to the ground in a fetal position, holding himself.

Varian stared open-mouthed at me; I couldn't help but smile. He smiled back, picked me up in his arms and we ran. More like he did the running. We went so fast, I couldn't see where we were going so I buried my face in his chest and enjoyed the ride.

When we finally stopped, I had no idea where we were, "Where are we?"

"Near the border."

"The US border?"

"Yes. We may have to go further."

"Why? Who was that?"

"That was the Voicer, the one who sent me here. He makes sure sentences are carried out and before you ask, I don't know what he's doing here," he answered.

"Something doesn't add up Varian," I said, "he was so angry with you. I thought he was going to kill you."

"He may have. Nice kick by the way," he smiled.

I giggled, "There's one tender area humans and Genesians have in common. Nice to know."

"Remind me not to make you angry," he quipped, "Come on, we should keep moving." He gathered me in his arms again and ran. As much as I was determined to watch which direction he took, I couldn't. He was too fast. When we stopped, I looked up to see the large letters, C.A.S.I.

"Varian, why are we here?"

"You said something didn't add up. I have a feeling Mr. Morgan didn't tell you everything. Has he been in contact with you?"

I shook my head.

"No he hasn't. It's been weeks since your last meeting. You should have heard something by now."

He was right. Maybe Hugh knew more than he said, "Ok, I think it's time to take a meeting," I said as I started for the entrance.

We entered the building and stood in the centre of the large foyer; all was quiet. Too quiet.

"I don't like this," I whispered.

"I'll check it out," Varian said. He was gone a few seconds and returned, "Deserted," he said.

"Hello?" I called out. A voice from an intercom answered, "Who's there?"

"Hugh, is that you? Where are you?"

"Carlynn!" Hugh answered, "I'm in sub-level 2. Take the elevator and push the green button. Hurry!"

The elevator door opened to another door, armored. I pressed the intercom button, "Hugh, it's me," the door opened. It must have been at least eighteen inches of solid steel, virtually impenetrable by human standards. Unless you tried with an atomic bomb.

We stepped in and the door closed behind. Hugh was there to meet us, "good to see a friendly face," he said with relief but he waned the instant he saw Varian, "What is he doing here?" he demanded, "Carlynn, he's dangerous. Are you mad? I've seen his kind in action. Not a pretty sight. I'm lucky to be alive."

"Calm down, Hugh," I said, "tell me what happened."

"Vampires, they came here and took everyone. I can only assume they're all dead," he was flustered, "I saw a big one attack the receptionist, dragged her off. The other, he moved so fast, I heard screams, then quiet. I survived, but only because I was the only one down here. I saw it all on the security cameras."

"When did this happen?" Varian asked.

"Yesterday," Hugh answered, "I haven't moved from here since, too afraid."

"The big one, was he bald?"

"Yes."

"And the other?"

"Dark, almost black eyes, black hair and pale complexion, like you. You're one of them, a vampire."

"Actually, I am Genesian," Varian corrected.

"What?" Hugh was confused.

"Varian," I interrupted, "you better tell Hugh what you told me."

30

Varian assured Hugh that the main level was safe and Hugh then agreed to accompany us up to the boardroom. I found a coffee maker in a small cabinet on the far wall of the room. Thankfully, coffee and filters were stored beside it. Taking the decanter, I left the room, found a tap in a tiny bathroom, filled the pot and returned. I needed a java jolt and had a feeling Hugh did too. I sat down, felt the tension between the two men. I looked back and forth at them, "Ok," I said, "what's with you two?"

Neither answered, they just stared at each other; Varian's expression of anger was very obvious. Hugh's, however, was of absolute terror.

"Hey!" I yelled, patience running low. The two finally turned toward me, "What's wrong now?" I demanded.

"Mr. Morgan has not been truthful with you Carlynn, I can feel it. He's hiding something," Varian revealed.

I turned toward Hugh, looked him straight in the eye, "Well?"

He turned away, rose from the chair and headed for the coffee, "Almost ready. Cream and sugar, Carlynn?"

Patience was gone, "Quit avoiding and tell us everything. Now."

Hugh returned to his seat and Varian took over coffee duty.

"The military hired us," he began, "they thought it would be better to use a private company such as C.A.S.I. and we were sworn to secrecy. S.E.T.I. discovered an anomaly that seemed to appear sporadically, however, always in the same area of space."

"How long have they known?" I asked.

"Several months."

"And they notified government officials," I finished.

"Yes."

Varian set a mug in front of Hugh and myself, "Has your government been in contact?" he asked.

"Yes."

"There's more," Varian said.

Hugh shifted in the seat, his fear apparent. "They've been communicating with two 'aliens'," he stopped, "Sorry," he apologized, "Genesians."

Varian shrugged.

Hugh continued, "A large bald man and a younger one, very similar to you in appearance."

I shot a glance at Varian. He knew what I was thinking as he thought the same.

"The larger one is the Voicer," Varian said, "and the other…Baxor perhaps?"

Hugh shook his head, "No, not Baxor. I thought I heard Jiz, Jaz?"

"Jez," Varian corrected, "his name is Jez Dorn.

Another friend from Genesia. You're sure of this?"

"Yes, but there were two more with them," Hugh informed, "the large…um Voicer, he seemed to be in charge."

"Varian, we should leave here," I urged. My intuition told me they were coming back soon. The idea of meeting up with a gang of vampires with only one to defend me and Hugh, I knew that would never work. We'd all die.

"Mr. Morgan. Have you a safe place to hide?" Varian asked, "They will be back, I promise you that."

"Yes I do."

"I will take you there. Carlynn and I will disappear and you will not see us again unless we seek you."

"I understand and thank you."

Varian smiled, "We are not that different from humans. Just like your race, we have some good ones and some bad ones," he offered his hand in friendship and Hugh took it.

I couldn't help but think of how lucky I was in finding Varian. Not that there weren't human men with the same qualities, I had just never met any. I could recall the four of us girls joking about how the kind of man we were looking for did not exist on earth. 'How was I to know my perfect match would be an alien?' I thought. Then I had another thought, '*Maybe the twins did know...*'

Valan pounded the walls with both fists to no avail. The protective glass was impenetrable, "Just leave it, Valan," Nemar said.

Valan lowered his arms, exhausted. He'd been pounding every inch of the glass, looking for any weakness in the structure.

A hint of laughter grew louder as the figure drew closer. A long black robe with silver embroidered circular emblems on each shoulder. The emblems shone brightly when the light hit them; it also indicated Valan's former colleague was behind the laughter.

"You're so angry, Valan," he said, "calm yourself. Don't let emotions rule you so."

"It's all I have, Balan," Valan snapped, "You've taken everything else, my position, my standing in Genesia and most of all, my son."

Balan circled the cell, "Ah yes, but your emotions are what got you here. If you'd only let go of Varian, mourn him, as if he'd died, you would have been able to move on. The council would have helped in your efforts to 'save face' and kept you on as a supreme judge. Instead," Balan's tone changed from jovial to dark, "instead you start digging for more answers, the truth, in your mind."

"You distorted the truth," Valan interrupted, "you framed my son!" Valan smashed his fists on the glass again.

31

"You need to keep your cool, Valan," Nemar urged, "Balan revels in your reaction."

"I'm trying my love. It's not that easy."

Nemar wrapped her arms around him and held tight, "We will find a way out of this," she promised.

Balan strolled down the long corridor, still smiling. His colleagues' reaction to seeing him surprised him, though he'd never show it. Valan knew more than he was supposed to and there was only one Genesian responsible for talking too much. His own son, Baxor. It was time to have a serious discussion with him. Explain to him that revealing the truth to others would put the whole operation they'd worked centuries on, in jeopardy.

Balan entered his office chamber, removed his cloak from his shoulders, and tossed it on the nearby chair. He sighed, sat behind the large marble desk, leaned back and closed his eyes.

'Baxor, this is your father. I need to see you now.'

Baxor was changing back to the uniform he usually wore while on Genesia. He quite liked the look and feel of the human fashions; it made him feel nostalgic. He was reminded of Genesia's history where the fashions were similar…a thousand years ago.

His mind picked up his father's request, more like an order. '*Uh oh*,' Baxor thought, '*he knows*.'

He made his way from the PTP to the waiting transport and climbed in. Voicer in the driver's seat turned, "You talk too much," he said.

Baxor had no reply. He was too busy thinking of what his father would do to him and what story he could come up with as an excuse. He'd have to tell his father the tall tale he'd told Varian and that Varian believed him. He'd explain that there was no threat and he'd conclude with the part of not being able to start life on a new planet without his best friend and seeing that it was his fault Varian was convicted in the first place, he wanted to make it up to him. Good. He would try it and hope his father would accept it.

He froze in front of the large office door. "Come in Baxor," he heard his father's voice, "I know you're there."

Baxor winced, turned the knob and stepped in, "You called?"

Balan was less than amused, "Sit. We need to discuss things once again."

"I know, I know," Baxor interrupted as sank into a plush leather chair, "I know that you know about Varian and his family."

"Oh? And what of the plan? The plan that has taken centuries to lay out and bring to fruition, Baxor? Have you forgotten?"

"No, I haven't."

"Then why, why would you do this?"

"You told me I had to leave this world behind soon. Start a new life on a new planet. How can I do that without my closest friends? They are like my family too, father."

"What have you told them?" Balan demanded.

"That Genesia is dying," he answered.

"Good. You cannot tell them the truth son. They will find out soon enough and even then, there may be repercussions. Not everyone will feel the way we do, Baxor. Once we are all on Earth, the ones who oppose the plan, they will have to die."

Baxor winced at the thought. Truth be known, he couldn't say for certain he agreed with the plan either, but he would never let his father know. *'What if he decides I'm a threat too?'* he thought. "I vow, I will keep the secret," he promised.

"See that you do."

"May I go now?"

Balan waved to his son to leave. He paced his office slowly, thinking how young Baxor was and his attachments to his closest friends. There would be no way to take everyone to Earth. They'd deplete the population too quickly. He hoped Baxor realized, now that he wanted

175

these people to make the journey, others would be stricken from the list. Perhaps it would be a good lesson for him to learn. He must accept the consequences of his actions.

Baxor made his way to his room, sat on his bed and thought, '*Am I really an evil person*?' The thought of using so many humans for one purpose and one only, food. He knew he had a flair for mischief, trouble making, but it was all in fun. His actions against Gengie Daj was necessary, an act of desperation. His father and the supreme judges deliberately left Varian and his family off the list; the reason – 'sympathizers.'

32

Hugh was safe, we hoped. Leaving the safety of the bunker, my cell rang. It was Lynn. It felt like years since I'd talked to her.

"Lynn. How are you? Where are you?"

Lynn giggled, "Slow down, Carlynn. I'm fine. Kaeton and I are in a town called Stein, um Steinb..."

"Steinbach?" I couldn't believe what I was hearing, "Really?"

"Yeah. Kaeton got bored in the city so we did some sightseeing and ended up here. Can you believe it?" she laughed.

I couldn't. If you want to go sightseeing, why not travel the country, the world, but to limit your travels to one Province?

"Lynn, you're not hunting or anything right? It's not a large city you know," I cautioned, "You don't want to draw attention."

"Relax," she answered, "I'm not hungry at all and I wouldn't…give me a little credit will you?"

"Sorry. I worry, you know."

"Yes, I know. Hey, can we meet?" she asked, "I mean, it's been ages and Kaeton says it's ok with him. In fact, he wants to talk to Varian anyway."

I relayed the message, Varian nodded. We agreed to meet the next evening.

The Days Inn. The largest hotel in the Steinbach area and the nicest. If you wanted expensive luxury, Winnipeg was the city to go to. It took years before the Days Inn was built. The town council thought it wasn't necessary to have such a large hotel in Steinbach. Another issue was liquor. The restaurant in the hotel wanted to serve alcoholic beverages and this was a dry town. Thankfully, time marched on, and Steinbach grew into a small city with a larger population, which in turn, prompted the provincial liquor commission to open a vendor. The small city was now wet.

We met Kaeton and Lynn in the restaurant. Great timing, since I was starving.

Lynn and I gave each other a huge bear hug, "Missed you," we both whispered at the same time. We giggled, "Some things never change," Lynn said. There were times we'd blurt out the same words in unison. We had that connection. I always considered Lynn the sister I never had.

We sat down, ordered drinks from an over-friendly waiter, I ordered a large garden salad and urged the others to order something so as to not draw attention to us. Plus, I felt a little self-conscious, being the only one ordering food.

"How is she coping?" Varian asked Kaeton.

Lynn was annoyed, "I'm right here. How about asking me how I'm doing?"

"Sorry," Varian apologized, "I know you're here, but Kaeton is your guardian and he keeps tabs on your progress as a newly joined. No offense intended, Lynn."

Lynn sat back in her seat, "Bloody wanker," she whispered.

I smiled, "Yep, some things never change." That made her smile.

I listened as Kaeton talked. It seemed as time went on, Lynn was able to tolerate the sunlight better. The sunscreen was starting to help but she had to limit her exposure to the sun. They were experimenting every day and every day it got better. The days between feedings were increasing also.

"I've been taking her into the woods to hunt instead of staying in the city," Kaeton said, "She's not happy with the change in diet, but blood is blood, no matter the species."

Kaeton smiled at Lynn, gently took her hand and kissed it like a medieval knight who just rescued the princess.

"Obviously, you two have grown close," I observed.

"Yes," both answered.

"Wow, not sure I expected that, given the history between you," I said.

"And some things do change, Carlynn," Lynn said and winked.

Adjusting to the newly found relationship between them, "Make sure you take care of her, always," I warned Kaeton.

He laughed, "And what could you possibly do to me?"

"I'll buy up all the sunscreen in the country if I have to," I barked, "see how you feel with a permanent severe sunburn."

"Ok, ok," Kaeton said, "don't worry. I don't intend to ever let her go."

"Good."

"There's more I need to tell you," Lynn's voice changed.

"What?"

"There's the funeral."

"Whose funeral?"

"Mine," she answered.

She explained how she and Kaeton set up the

scenario of her death. It was a simple malady, anaphylactic shock, an allergic reaction to a bee sting. She'd never been stung before, so no one knew of an allergy.

"You should have told me. I would have been there," I sympathized.

"We didn't have a lot of time to do it," Lynn said, "my family could never see me like this; I had to 'die'. It was hard seeing my parents mourn. It took all my will not to jump up, hug them tightly, and show that I was alive and well, but I couldn't. This was the only solution. Better than them thinking that I was missing indefinitely. They had to have closure."

All I could do was nod and wonder if I could do the same to my parents.

"Sorry you had to go through that, Lynn," Varian said.

"Cheers."

"Let's change the subject, shall we?" I said, trying to lighten the mood. Varian's smile faded, "Time to go," he said as he grabbed my hand. We met Kaeton and Lynn behind the hotel, "What took you?" Kaeton was irritated. I looked away biting my lip, "Oh, sorry, Carlynn," he quickly apologized. I nodded.

"Kaeton, did you recognize any of them?" Varian asked.

"No, I just know they're from home."

"I wonder if they've started transporting already," Varian whispered, "it's too soon."

"I thought Baxor was going to inform you when it would start," I said.

"We need to contact him."

"How?"

"I know a place. It should be safe enough to return by now," Varian glanced my way, "Don't worry they'll never know."

"I'm going to hold you to that statement," I warned.

33

Going back to the farm was risky. We could have been seen by my parents, my dad in particular. He didn't have a set schedule when he walked his property line, checking fences. What if he spotted us on one of his treks? What if mom decided to join him? I told myself to shut up and trust the man I was with.

We arrived at my star landing site, where Varian pulled out his cell and motioned for Kaeton to do the same.

He wired them together, "Let's hope Baxor is listening," he said to Kaeton. He was. No 'Hello,' or 'How are you?' He sounded a bit panicked.

"My father and the supreme judges are watching me closely, Var. They know I gave you information and they're not happy."

"My parents, are they OK?" Varian asked.

"They are fine. Safe, but I fear I'll need to expedite my plan," he could sense fear in Baxor.

"Why, what's wrong?"

"Father doesn't trust me anymore, hence the constant chaperone," Baxor said with contempt, "It wasn't easy, but I've managed to give him the slip. I'm sure he's searching as we speak."

"Let me come back to help you," begged Varian.

"Not yet my friend, it's too dangerous. The Voicer's been at the PTP console almost constantly," Baxor said, "I'm just outside the room. He doesn't know I'm here and I'm hoping he'll leave soon. Stay where you are and I'll contact you as soon as I can."

"For how long?"

"I don't know. You'll have to be patient. It could be

a while," the connection was cut.

Varian sighed, "OK, you heard Baxor. You may as well get comfortable and hope it's not too long."

We sat around the hole as if it were a campfire, without the flames. Me being the only one getting cold, and Varian being the consummate gentleman, he put his jacket around my shoulders and pulled me closer to him. I used my imagination since he had no body heat to offer and yet I warmed up nicely.

We engaged in idle chit chat for about half an hour when the cells went off.

"We have very little time, Varian. If you want to come back here, it has to be now. Voicer was called away," Baxor left almost no chance for a reply.

"I'm ready," Varian replied.

"Wait, wait!" I shouted, "When will you be back?"

"I'm not sure, Carlynn."

"But you will be back…"

"I can't guarantee your safety, Varian," Baxor injected.

"You have to!" my voice cracked.

"Sorry, Carlynn," Baxor offered condolences,

"Varian, come on."

"I'll be back, I promise," he vowed, "Kaeton, Lynn, take care of her."

"Will do, Var," Kaeton promised.

Varian jumped down in the hole, "Ready."

"No!" I cried.

"I love you, Carlynn," he said

"No, you can't leave me," I screamed, and jumped in with him just as the transport began. Kaeton and Lynn stood in shock, neither expecting this to happen. Hell I didn't expect my own reaction. I just knew I couldn't let Varian go. Not now when we had just found one another.

"Carlynn, it's too dangerous for you." Varian said but there was no way I was going to be left behind, "Bax, stop the transport!" he shouted.

"Too late Var, I stop now and it could be weeks before I get another shot at it," Baxor said.

"But..."

He couldn't protest anymore, the transport had begun and I hung on to him with all my strength.

"I did not see that coming," Lynn said, "I mean...wow."

"Ditto," Kaeton whispered.

I felt dizzy, weightless, a total loss of control. I didn't know if I still had my arms around Varian. I couldn't breath – lights like strobes, a black hole.

"Grab her and let's go, Varian," a harsh whisper, but I couldn't open my eyes.

34

THE PLAN

"I think I understand why my father may not trust me anymore."

"Don't beat yourself up," Varian said, "I asked and you being the man you are, you acted on impulse as usual. Not always bad." He smiled at his best friend who put himself on the line by his actions.

"Why would I beat myself up?"

"Human expression."

"Ah."

"My parents, where are they?" Varian was clearly anxious.

"Slow down, Varian. If we rush into anything, we put all of our lives at risk. We need a plan," Baxor said, "a plan that keeps you out of sight. If any other Genesian sees you…"

"Yes, I know," he agreed.

"And her," Baxor pointed, "Complication."

"Yeah."

"She loves you."

"Yes."

"And you love her."

"Yes."

"Varian in love with a human. Who would have seen that coming," Baxor smiled.

"Hey guys."

The two jolted and turned, "I'm still here," my voice rough, groggy. I sat up, trying to clear my head. A few seconds and the blur was gone, "Where am I?" I looked around a large room, a bedroom. The walls were smooth silver-gray with flecks…granite. This is a cave.

"You're in my home," Baxor answered.

"You live in a cave," I said.

"All Genesian's homes are meticulously carved out of the rock. We have no trees here, not any more. We adapted."

"I made it! I'm on Genesia!" I jumped and ran into Varian's arms. He fell over, "Hey," he laughed, "take it easy!"

"Shhhhh!" Could you two be any louder? You're not supposed to be here, remember?"

"Sorry," we both whispered.

Baxor opened the door, peeked out to see if anyone detected the noise. Nothing. Good and he shut the door. Then he froze for a second, "Wait, how can you possibly push Varian over? You're a human. Weak."

"Thanks," my sarcasm evident.

Varian asked, "How do you feel?"

"Great! Never better."

Varian and Baxor looked confused, "Atmosphere?" one asked, and the other shrugged, "Who knows. It's not that different from Earth's. We have more oxygen. Maybe that's it."

"Um, guys," I interrupted, "I really don't think we have time to debate this. Baxor, I'd punch you but since you're the reason I know Varian and we need you to save his family, I'll pardon you."

"Really…you'd punch me?"

I could think of no other way to test my hypotheses and punched him in the stomach.

"Ooooomph," and he was on his knees.

"Wow," Varian marveled.

Now that I proved my point, "Time to focus," I said, "We need a plan." We had made it out of the PTP room just in time. The Voicer came back to keep an eye on it and he had no idea Baxor brought us back. Thankfully, Baxor knew the code to reverse the sabotage. We wouldn't be harmed during transport.

"There's no way of knowing when I'll get the chance again. It could be days," he said.

"We have to figure something out. A way that will save my parents and get us all out of here at the same time. Bax, after all this and if we get away, your father, will he condemn you?" Varian asked.

"Yes, yes, he will," he answered.

"He won't know you're the one helping us," I said.

"He will suspect me, Carlynn. That will be enough in his eyes."

"He wouldn't harm you. You're his son," I said, instilling the parental protection of any father.

Baxor didn't answer, instead Varian spoke, "Why the change, Bax?"

"Let's just say I'm doubting my father's and the supreme judge's plan for us. For all Genesia. We'll discuss this later. Let's see if we can get your family."

We spent what seemed like hours, discussing different scenarios in rescuing Varian's parents. All ended badly. Finally, I suggested it was possible we were over thinking it and maybe we needed to keep things as simple as possible. One major obstacle was the Voicer. I really didn't want to deal with him again. Didn't think I'd be too lucky the second time.

The sun on the horizon of Genesia was a sight. It was huge compared to that of Earth's. For a moment I thought it would overcome the planet and we would all fry.

I was over reacting but who wouldn't? I'm the first to travel to another planet, another solar system!

Right?

Then I noticed something I'd never seen before. Varian yawned, so did Baxor. They were actually sleepy and I wasn't.

"You two need to rest," I said, "I'll keep watch. We'll talk more when you wake."

The two nodded and closed their eyes. What a strange sight. It made me wish I had my camera. Both stood, eyes closed, fast asleep…I remembered my cell.

Kodak moment.

35

UH OH

I watched Varian and Baxor sleep peacefully. The two reminded me of department store mannequins; they looked like them too.

Genesians are the most beautiful race I've ever seen, albeit similar to each other in appearance. All dark, raven hair, very dark, almost black eyes, skin like porcelain. The men all had handsome, chiseled features. I hadn't seen any females yet, but I assumed they were as beautiful as the men were handsome. A little un-nerving for a mere human. And the perfect smiles they all possessed. Evolutionary I'm sure, as their teeth were no longer needed for chewing their food, they simply punctured their victims. The time would come when Varian and I would have opportunity to discuss the effects of the Genesian's bite. The one detail I knew is the bite must kill the prey or they became comatose and eventually died. I wanted to know if that slow death was painful or peaceful and exactly how did they 'join' someone? Their weapons, I found them completely fascinating. From what I'd gathered in examining Vlad's skull, the front row retracted and a row behind moved forward into position. When the deed was done, the process reversed and the front row returned to perfect, pearly whites. Vlad's skull reminded me of a shark's jawbone. The difference being, sharks have multiple rows of teeth whereas Genesians have two rows. Although, to be absolutely sure, I'd have to examine other Genesians. I could ask Varian. I'd have immense joy examining his mouth.

Did I hear something? No, couldn't be. I relaxed a bit, the door opened, "Baxor darling, are you coming? We must be there when your father comes out."

I froze as this beautiful, raven-haired woman entered. She couldn't have been more than thirty years old. Was this his mother? His girlfriend or wife? She spotted me, "Who are you?"

'*Uh oh*,' I thought and made an attempt to get the deer in the headlights expression off my face, "Um, hi, I'm Carlynn Willows. A friend of Baxor's."

She stared at me, "You don't belong here, Carlynn Willows," she said, angrily.

"Mom, hey!' Baxor chimed in. I'm not going to lie; I was elated when I heard that voice. It meant the two were awake, but it was too late. She was not going to listen to her son, I could sense it.

"She's a friend," Baxor immediately defended.

"From Earth," his mother snapped, "How did she get here and what's he doing here?" she pointed at Varian.

"I can explain," Baxor said.

"No you can't son. You don't know what you've done. You have condemned yourself. You may have put your father and me in danger as well. Has anyone else seen you?"

"No," he answered, "just you. Father doesn't know either."

"Keep it that way. You must leave...now!" she commanded.

"We can't," Varian spoke, "the Voicer still controls the PTP."

"Silence, murderer! How dare you speak to me!" she was on the verge of screaming.

My instincts drove my feet forward toward the woman, "Back off, bitch!"

"You dare speak to me, you insect," She spewed, "you are a weak, insignificant speck...FOOD!"

"Mother!"

"Let's go," Varian said as he took my hand and headed for the door. Baxor's mother stepped in front, "You," she pointed at me, "you may not leave."

I turned to Baxor, "Sorry Bax, I have to," I apologized and threw all my strength into my fist that connected with her cheek.

She went down hard. "Carlynn!" Baxor shouted.

"I said sorry."

"How…never mind," Baxor was shaken, "We have to go before she recovers," he closed the door behind us and locked it. He saw the look I had, "My parents used to lock me in for safety. That's what they told me anyway."

"Why would you need protection?"

"My father, being a supreme judge, they always had a fear I'd be harmed in some way," he said.

"I thought Genesians were past that, evolved?"

"Yeah, parents…you know. My theory is they wanted to keep me from getting into trouble. I was the mischievous type, right Var?"

"Understatement," Varian quipped.

"Har, har."

We followed Baxor to a door labelled 'Restricted,' he opened it and let us through. "Follow me," he ordered and led us through a maze of corridors. Had I been on my own, I would have been lost for weeks, my sense of direction being what it is…terrible.

Another door, 'Restricted,' Baxor opened it quietly, "Keep quiet," he whispered. We entered and he made us stay by the door. He was gone for a moment and when he returned, he took Varian aside. They spoke for a short time, I saw a smile get wider and wider on him, '*That could only mean one thing,*' I thought.

"Ok, Carlynn," Varian said, "here we go. You can't say anything. We have to keep silent, if any monitors pick up voices, it will activate security." I nodded, thinking what a strange security system they had. The room was bare, no furniture, but lit up with bright lights that I couldn't see. What I did see was a large glass box in the middle of the room, two people within it. There was no mistake, they were Varian's parents. The woman stood, pressed her hands to the glass, tears streaming down her cheeks. The man behind her with his arms wrapped around his wife, the same. I could see features on Varian that both parents possessed. Varian touched the glass; no words were said.

Baxor pulled Varian away, we stood back as he exposed a panel on the wall. He entered a complex code and the glass wall lifted.

"Now!" Baxor whispered.

We all ran for the back door. Baxor leading the way down yet another long corridor that led us back to the PTP room. Was everything on this planet connected?

"We'll have to rush him," Baxor said when he saw the Voicer still monitoring the transport. We all agreed and that's when an alarm started, "Shit," I said.

The others looked at me, "Sorry, habit…Earth expression."

"Now!" Baxor yelled. We knocked the door down. The Voicer stood by the PTP, weapons bared, eyes black as night. He was huge. How were we going to overpower this massive being?

"Traitors!" he yelled and started toward us, but the others were fast. Baxor, Varian, the parents all surrounded him and took hold of his limbs, but he was strong. All of them struggled to hold him, "What now?" Varian called out, still holding an arm with all his strength. Baxor shouted, "Carlynn!" I looked at him, "You'll have to do it!"

"Me, how? I'm human," I was scared to death, not sure I could even move a muscle.

"We can't let go," Varian said, "You will have to try."

I couldn't believe they expected me to do anything

to stop this mass, "What do I do?" I asked.

"The only thing that will stop him," Varian responded, "Remember?"

I thought for a moment then realized, "Are you serious?"

"Yes!" Varian and Baxor shouted in unison.

I took a short moment to psych myself up for the impossible task. As I approached the Voicer, "Food!" he spewed, "You aren't anything but food." That was enough to piss me off. I stepped back a bit and lunged at the huge figure, straight for the chest. The loud crack felt deafening to me. I could feel the warm liquid, the large organ I wrapped my fingers around and yanked as hard as possible. The Voicer's body was instantly limp. They let him fall to the floor. I stood staring at his heart still in my hand, unable to believe what I'd just done. I took a life. Yes, he was a horrible being, not even human, but a living being all the same and I ended that life.

"Carlynn," Varian spoke softly, "let it go," he loosened my grip on the organ and it fell to the floor. I felt those strong arms wrap around me, "It's ok, don't cry."

I didn't realize I was crying.

The other voices in the room, they sounded like distant murmurs; something about Earth, the transport system, sabotage. Before I knew it, we were 'traveling' again.

THINGS CHANGE

Five people crawled out of my star landing hole. One human and four Genesians. It was dark outside.

"It's about bloody time!" Lynn's voice broke the silence as she emerged from the shadows, Kaeton close behind, "You've been gone three days! I was worried sick!"

"Sorry," I gave her a hug, "didn't feel like three days. Lynn, it was so incredible, going through, the other side and the whole process. It changed my physical strength. I've never felt so good!"

"That's great," she said, but she was looking at me as though I was a virtual stranger.

"What? What's wrong?" I asked as the clouds in the night sky made their way past the bright full moon that lit up the darkness.

"Varian," Lynn called for him to come closer and he obliged. His face said it, something was definitely wrong with me.

"Lynn, give me a mirror," I said holding my hand out.

"Maybe not quite yet, Carlynn," she delayed.

"Lynn...now!" I ordered.

She reached into her Prada, took out a compact and slowly handed it to me. I opened it. My reflection, it was me with an obvious change. I had aged, a lot. "Varian," I heard myself whisper before fainting.

Distant voices getting louder, "Carlynn!" I could feel someone shaking me, calling my name, touching my cheek, "Wake up please."

I opened my eyes slowly, "Wow," Varian helped me up, "did I just dream that?"

"No, Carlynn," a voice I hadn't heard before which could only be Valan, Varian's father. He came closer, "I'm Valan and this is Nemar. You know who we are."

I nodded.

"What happened to me?"

"An effect of the PTP I'm afraid. It's the only explanation," he answered, "In addition to you being human, different solar systems. It could be many things."

"How do we fix it?" Varian asked.

"Not sure we can, son."

"Wait," I interrupted, "I'm 22 years old and I just aged 20 years in a few seconds. You're telling me this is permanent?"

"I don't know. Give it some time. The travel effects may correct themselves as you adjust back to Earth's atmosphere."

"But you're not certain," I pushed.

"No."

Like a deflated balloon, I felt my body slouch and I

sat down on the hard ground, shoulders sagged, face in hands. I cried.

"I'm sorry," Varian apologized.

I shook my head, "Not your fault."

Lynn sat next to me, consoling, while the others discussed what the next move should be.

"There has to be a place we can go where we'll be safe. Where Carlynn will be safe too," Varian said.

"The cabin," I suggested, "the Voicer was the only one who knew about it right?"

"As far as I know," he answered.

"Then it's settled, the cabin it is."

We agreed to meet at the cabin in the morning. Kaeton and Lynn took Valan and Nemar hunting and Varian and I headed back to the Days Inn where I had parked my car. It was still there, which surprised me. I thought it may have been towed, having been there for so long when I never checked in.

I let Varian drive as I wasn't up to it. I felt so tired – aging in a few seconds sure took its toll on me. A gradual process taking years, the affects come on slowly as we humans feel the aches and pains, the hair starts to gray slightly, the small wrinkles pop up, giving a preview of what's to come. I had a strong urge to contact my mom and tell her I really understood what she meant when she talked about growing older and yet still feeling young at heart. There was no way she could see me now. I looked her age and I looked just like her.

"You're beautiful, Carlynn."

"How…can you read my thoughts?"

"No, I feel you. I feel your fear about looking older than you are and I need you to know you will always be beautiful to me."

"I'm older."

"Through no fault of yours."

"But…"

"Don't worry about something that's out of our control right now. Please relax, try to get some sleep."

I closed my eyes thinking I wouldn't be able to sleep. I was wrong.

I awoke in the familiar bed; we were back at the cabin. I sat up and stretched my arms above my head, rubbed my eyes. Nature called and I answered. Washing my hands, I had a look in the mirror. My gasp was involuntary.

"Carlynn, you awake?" Varian called out.

"Yeah, yeah I am," I answered, "Don't come in here."

Varian entered the bathroom. I managed a weak smile, "Hey".

He smiled, "Hey."

"Still look old."

"Ok, I'm feeling a little insulted now," he said, "You know how old I am?"

"But you still look so young."

"We will figure this out, Carlynn."

I nodded, "Ok."

"Come on, I made coffee for you and my parents are waiting to have a proper visit with you," his voice lightened.

Everyone was in the living room chatting when I walked in. Nemar rose and gave me a hug, "Varian has told us so much about you, I feel I've always known you," she said.

"Thank you."

I joined the gathering. The discussion being more

for Valan and Nemar's education of the conditions on Earth. Although they seemed to know a lot already, there were some things they didn't know, such as the effects of joining a human, the sunlight, the anti-aging, (I called that a bonus).

"There are benefits to a longer lifespan, yes," Valan commented, "but there are detriments as well."

Lynn interrupted, "I can't speak for a Genesian, but as a human who has recently joined, I'll tell you this, I watched my family and friends mourn my 'death' and they got off easy. I'm the one who will mourn them, watching as slowly, one by one, they die, until there is no one left."

As if Lynn just realized her future, she excused herself and stepped outside the cabin door. I was about to follow when Kaeton touched my hand, "Let me go," he said. I agreed.

The door closed.

37

SACRIFICE

"Baya!" Balan shouted, "Wake up. What happened to you?"

She got up and rubbed her cheek, "The human."

"What human?"

"The one I caught with Varian and our son in this very room. I was going to let them go with the condition that no one see them."

"Why would you do that?"

"Baxor and Varian," she answered, "I would have let them leave, but not the human…she hit me."

"And you fell? Impossible!"

"Apparently not, Balan," Baya countered, "She's human and she overpowered me. Very unsettling."

"Baxor brought them here, didn't he?" Balan assumed.

"Yes."

He couldn't believe his own son would betray him like this. Betrayed his own kind and put the whole plan in jeopardy. He had to meet with the rest of the supreme judges so they could prepare a plan. He knew he had to reveal who the leak was and it would be difficult to convince them that he had nothing to do with it. He had to turn his back on his own son, condemn him. It was a sacrifice he had to make in order to save face.

Baxor as good as signed his own death warrant.

It was as Balan predicted. Baxor was condemned to death by the judges. They would send an envoy of assassins to Earth, hunt Baxor and any accomplices, and end their lives. Balan and Baya were confined to their home for the time being. A precaution just in case they had a change of heart and tried to warn their son.

Baya lay in bed, sobbing uncontrollably, "What have we done?"

"We saved our race."

"We killed our own son!" she screeched.

"A sacrifice necessary for the rest of us to survive," his justification began to sound weak, even to him.

"You think I don't know?" she knew her husband thought she was a bit of an airhead, a materialistic, selfish, socialite, "Once again, you and your judges underestimate my intelligence. What we've accomplished in the Alpha system has nothing to do with our survival and you know it."

Balan charged his wife, pushed her against the wall, hand on her chest, "Don't push me," he threatened but Baya was not about to back down this time. She'd always followed his lead but enough was enough. She pushed back throwing Balan against the opposite wall, "I'll push as hard as I want and you will not stop me," she hissed.

"Baya!"

"There's an Earth saying I've wanted to use but never had the opportunity before...piss off!" she left their bedroom.

She'd have to find a way out of this confinement and away from him. The years spent by his side as a supporting wife, doting on his every whim, always giving off appearances, that was over now.

Balan never knew how many times he thought his wife was well out of ear shot, when she wasn't. She tired of being the kept woman of a supreme judge. She also tired of being excused from the room and though she was in agreement of the plan, it was not her intention to stand by her husband's side as it was executed. She would go to Earth and be her own person. The new complication was her willful son, who brought a human into her home. She would have let Varian go, but the human, she smelled so good. She wanted to sink her teeth into the blood she hadn't tasted for centuries. When the aroma caught her senses, she was instantly reminded of the taste of real, undiluted blood; real food. Her hunger grew at the thought and she had no choice but to reach for the substitute. 'You won't have to put up with this much longer,' she thought as she downed a large bottle of thick liquid.

"Baya."

She turned, teeth bared, eyes black - Balan.

38

"PERHAPS WE DESTROY THE PTP?"

"You know that's not possible my dear."

Varian's parents whispered to each other, searching for solutions to a problem that was bigger than any human would ever know. Except for me, of course, but I didn't know either. The only thing I knew at the moment was that I was the only human in the room. I could say Lynn was human, or at least she used to be, but not anymore. She was a vampire now.

"Genesian," a voice from behind me corrected.

"What?" I turned to see Rae's smiling face, "Hey there," she greeted.

"Rae!" I threw my arms around her, "I've missed you. Where's Jade?"

"Right here," Jade stepped through the door. She started to say something when I grabbed her and pulled her into a circle of hugging. When I finally let go, Jade laughed, "Great to see you too!" she said.

"You ok, Carlynn? You look tired," Rae observed, "I know it's been a while since we've seen each other, but you look like you've been in a rough battle and lost."

"No offense," Jade finished her sister's statement.

"None taken," I said, "How are you two even here?"

"We are Genesian," a duo response.

"When you disappeared with Varian through the PTP, Lynn called us."

"You knew?" I asked Lynn with a look that said, 'How could you not tell me?'

"Yes."

"Before you get upset at Lynn for not telling you, I am the one to blame," Kaeton stepped in, "I sought them out when Lynn was joined. I needed help and…"

"You know each other pretty well, I'd say," I said.

"Rae, Jade, it's time you tell her everything," Nemar gave the twins no option to hide who they really were anymore.

"Everyone please have a seat. This will take a while," Jade opened, "Carlynn, Rae and I are Genesian. We've been on Earth for centuries and before you start your vast list of queries," she smiled that fanged familiar smile, "let us finish our story." She knew me too well.

"We came here to escape persecution because our parents didn't agree with the 'plan' the supreme judges and the Voicer had developed. Rae and I were very young at the time, about fifteen years old in Earth years. Had we stayed on Genesia, our family would have been killed."

Rae took over, "Earth isn't really a prison, it's a newly developed source for Genesia."

"A source for what?" I had to interject.

"A food source, to put it bluntly. We, Genesians I mean, we are the ones who seeded the Earth. We developed your race for one purpose…food. There is no such thing as a 'substitute' for blood. It's always been human blood, just diluted a bit so it would go farther. So, all those stories you hear about alien abductions are true for the most part. With the exception of a few nuts that relish the attention for claiming to be abducted. There is no such thing as a food shortage or a planet that is dying. Humans have been our food source for almost a million years."

"Wait," Baxor interrupted, "how do you know all this? My father…"

"Your father lied," Jade cut him off, "We could go on with many more details but I think this is enough for now."

"And the convicts sent here?" my turn to ask questions.

"Some really are convicts, but most are watchers. They keep an eye on you humans and do their best to stop you from destroying yourselves." Rae answered, "Earth was a simple alternative to send law breakers, rather than keep them on Genesia. Cheaper, really, plus they acted as guinea pigs for the judges. They fed on the humans.

Testing the blood so to speak, see if anything has changed through your evolution."

"If we destroy ourselves?"

"Then Genesia really will be in trouble. We will turn on each other as we did in the past and eventually will render ourselves extinct," Valan announced.

"Earth is a farm?" it was my turn to be blunt.

"A crude way to put it, but yes," Rae said.

"Again, I have to ask," Baxor insisted, "How do you know of this all?"

Rae and Jade looked at each other, "Our parents are the scientists who seeded Earth," they answered.

"Holy shit," Lynn whispered.

"And where are they now? Why didn't they come with you tonight?" I asked.

"They're dead," Rae answered, "the Voicer..." her voice cracked.

"If it's any consolation, the Voicer is dead," Varian offered.

"How?" Jade asked.

Varian pointed at me.

"You?"

I nodded. Varian told the story in detail as the twins listened intently and when he finished the two embraced me in such a tight hug I could hardly breathe.

"How can we ever thank you?" Rae said.

"Not necessary, really," I said, "I'm not sure how I feel about it right now. I took a life."

"You did more good than you realize," Jade justified.

I shrugged and walked away. Rae was about to follow when Varian stopped her, "Let me."

39

PUT ON THE SPOT

I took a nap that evening. I was so exhausted from recent events I could hardly keep my eyes open. It was far from restful. An array of dreams haunted my so-called rest. Dreams of an onslaught of Genesians flooding through the PTP and attacking humans, then jumping to a once beautiful beach, littered with blood and bodies. Men, women and children, all brutally sucked dry and left to rot. The final scene was of me going back to the farm to visit, only to find mom and dad sitting on the sofa, motionless in front of a blaring television, Duke laying at their feet, all dead. I awoke screaming and Varian was at my side in a flash.

"Bad dream?" he whispered, while holding me tightly.

"Yeah."

"It's just that, a dream. Nothing more. Come…join us in the living room. We've been putting things together and…well, just come."

"OK."

"We can't stay together like this. It won't be long before my father and the judges send their so-called law keepers after us."

"You mean assassins, don't you?" Valan corrected.

"In all probability, yes," Baxor answered.

"So we have to fight back," I said.

"There's only a few of us and who know how many others, already here, have been ordered to kill us on sight," Varian said, "Then…"

"And then we start dying, one-by-one," I injected.

"Humans don't have to die!" Rae snapped and everyone's attention turned to her, "Rae!" Jade scolded, "Now may not be the time!"

"When will it be time, Jade?" Rae shot back, "We can feed on humans without killing or joining. Our family practiced this for centuries. It took some time but we have mastered the technique."

"How is it Genesians don't know about it?" Nemar asked.

"The supreme judges did know," Jade said as she looked to Valan.

"Dad?"

Valan sighed, "We were informed of the technique but decided it was too risky. There was a slight possibility the victim would be joined instead. At the time, we couldn't take the chance. It would mean more Genesians added to the population. Earth's population. Imagine this happening over and over until it consumes the planet."

"Valan, you knew the plan!" Nemar couldn't believe her own husband allowed it. To go this far, "Who are you?"

"It was humans or my family! The other judges didn't give me a choice and I will always choose my family," Valan was angry, he was frustrated and he was hungry. He turned to me, his weapons ready.

"Dad!"

Valan looked to his son, "Dad, time to go for a walk…now. Jade, Rae, will you join us please?"

The twins followed Varian and his father out the door.

Nemar sat next to me, "He wouldn't have hurt you."

"You sure about that?" I asked

"Yes I am," she answered, then said, "You didn't even flinch when he looked your way. You are not afraid of us."

"No I'm not."

"Why?"

"Not a lot scares Carlynn," Lynn said, "right, Car?"

"Right."

The mood lightened, everyone relaxed and engaged in small talk, although Baxor did express his curiosity of feeding without killing, hoping the twins would return soon so the procedure could be explained.

"We've waited this long, we can wait a few minutes more Bax," Kaeton said.

An hour passed when they finally returned, walking in laughing, joking, as if nothing had happened just an hour before.

Valan approached, "Carlynn, I am sorry I let my anger get the best of me, it will not happen again."

"Thank you."

"I'm glad we're all friends again," Varian said as he pulled me close to him, "We did it, Carlynn."

"Did what?"

"We fed without killing."

I looked at the twins, "You showed them? Are you sure they're ok? Did they feel pain?"

"Slow down!" Rae laughed, "No harm or pain came to anyone."

I was relieved but conflicted. It was apparent that Genesians and humans would be forever connected; they were, in fact, our ancestors – parents. Geez, if our own ancestors saw them thousands of years ago, they may have seen them as gods...or demons. That is if a Genesian was seen in mid feed.

Vampires were coming, a lot of them. How were we going to defend ourselves? They were millions of years more advanced in every way. Maybe our leaders could negotiate with them. Maybe even help to find an alternative to human blood. Varian did say animal blood would suffice in a pinch, but human blood was still needed in the end. There were more questions than answers and I needed answers. More importantly, I needed time to find those answers, "Baxor."

"Yeah."

"The PTP, can it be disabled?"

"I would think so."

"We have to disable it so the migration won't begin."

"There's more than one PTP. How do you propose we do this?" Baxor asked, then said, "And even if we do that, it won't be long before they're up and running again."

"But it will slow them down. Give us time."

"Time for what?" Lynn chimed in.

"Time to figure out how we can survive, Lynn," I snapped.

"Bloody hell. Sorry I asked."

"No, I'm sorry," I stressed.

"May I offer a solution?" All eyes landed on Nemar, "Well don't look so surprised! The solution is for Carlynn only."

"Mother, no!"

"Son, it may be the only thing to save her."

"We don't know the long term effects of joining a human. Kaeton has kept Lynn safe, taught her our ways, but result of the joining differs from what we are. For example, the exposure to UV rays," Varian explained.

"But that is improving Var," Kaeton reminded.

"Yes, but has she developed to the point where only sunscreen is needed?"

"No," he answered, "but she may."

"Again, I say we don't know long term affects," Varian reiterated.

I listened as they debated my fate and thought, *'Interesting, they haven't asked me how I feel about it.'* I laughed quietly to myself.

"How about we discuss this at a later date and concentrate on Carlynn's suggestion," Valan broke in, "If we consider disabling the PTPs, we'll have to break into four pairs. That means we all go back."

Valan came over to me, took my hand, "You can't come this time my dear. You'll need to stay here. Besides, I don't know what another trip will do to you."

"Wait, you're going to leave me here alone?" I couldn't believe what I was hearing, "Varian?"

GOING BACK

Everyone gathered in the pit once more, everyone but me. I found out there are actually four PTPs on Genesia. The one I had gone through was the main one. Their destinations all differed with machines located on the far corners of the planet. Lynn, being the newest Genesian, was paired with Baxor instead of Kaeton. The general feeling was that he could keep her safer as Kaeton was considered a criminal where they were going.

He wasn't crazy about leaving his new love with Baxor, that was obvious, "You'd better take care of her, Bax," he said.

"I will," Baxor said with a broad smile, "You worry too much."

"I have reason to," Kaeton replied, his gaze on Lynn lingered and she returned the look.

The twins were nervous, yet excited to be going back. It had been so long, they wondered if a lot had changed. It was too bad their trip back would be a short one and would they be able to disable the PTP chosen for them?

"How do you come back with the PTPs not working?" I asked. I was so afraid I'd never see any of them again. What if they were caught? Or killed? I just found the love of my life and I could lose him. I knelt beside the hole, he kissed me goodbye, "I'll be back," he promised.

"I've heard that before," I managed a weak smile and they were gone.

I sat and cried – for how long, I don't know.

Finally, I rose and went to the small campsite Varian set up for me. No one knew how long they'd be gone, so he decided to make it as comfortable as possible for me.

I had the newest and best tent available, blankets that kept a person warm, even in the coldest of temperatures, a small gas barbeque, lamps, two flashlights and food. Pretty much everything I needed. I agreed to camp out for a maximum of four days. If they weren't back by then, I was ordered to leave the area for fear of being spotted by any watchers or assassins, now certain to be searching for them.

I hated camping! I always said my idea of a holiday was a Best Western, with all the conveniences. Not roughing it. I'd have never done this for anyone else but Varian. Sigh, '*ok, I may as well make some supper.*'

The dusk grew dark quickly as I slowly ate the baked beans, wieners and a slice of rye bread, '*a true camper's meal,*' I thought. The camp fire burned slow and steady and I found myself gazing at the stars. Wondering if I could spot the one Varian was on right now. A small transistor radio sat beside my tent. I found a talk show station whose topic for the evening was UFOs and whether ET really existed. I laughed quietly at some of the callers who claimed they had been abducted, these were the obvious nuts, but there was one caller I listened very carefully to. He was calm and collected, didn't change his demeanor in any way, even when the host tried to make fun of him. Before the caller hung up, he had one last warning, "'They're coming." The host mimicked the warning, "They're coming folks! Beware, you cannot hide!" He laughed. I changed the station. That last caller gave me an uneasy feeling. 'He knows,' I thought, wondering who he was. Looking up at the night sky again, I saw a falling star. How I wanted it to be my friends coming back to me. Especially Varian.

Inside the tent, curled up in the thickest sleeping bag I'd ever seen, on the air mattress, toasty and warm, I had to admit I was quite comfortable. I still had trouble sleeping though, waking several times during the night. It was so quiet in the woods, no traffic noises, no ambulance or police sirens, no sounds of excited chatter or laughter on the street. Familiar sounds I'd grown accustomed to when I lived in the city. Back in the country, I remembered the silence. Well, there was the odd chirp of a cricket looking for a suitable mate, or the hoot of an owl, and even the croaking frogs in the distant swamp. Still, too quiet for me.

I must have fallen asleep again because I awoke to daylight outside my tent. I crawled out to a beautiful, cool, crisp morning with a little frost on the ground. I headed straight for the fire pit, stacked the wood, added a bit of kindling and lit it up. Within minutes I had a nice little fire going and I sat by it, warming up fast.

I was still alone. '*They aren't back yet,*' I thought. '*It's only been twelve hours. Lynn told me we were gone for three days so I have no reason to panic yet.*' I kept telling myself, '*Two more days, two more days, two more days.*' It didn't work very well.

Another long day of waiting, going for short walks, not wanting to travel too far from the star landing, reading, playing games on my phone and I even tried to get a hold of Hugh Morgan. No luck.

Dusk was falling on day two and to say that I wasn't worried would be a gross understatement. I made my way back to the star pit, sat at the edge and waited. Nothing else to do anyway. That's when it flashed and two figures stood in the hole, Valan and Kaeton. The two climbed out to my extended arms grabbing each for a welcome back hug, "So glad to see you," I said, "how did it go?"

"Ok, I think. I'm hoping our little bomb worked," Kaeton answered. Another flash, Rae and Jade hopped out, "Done and done!" Rae announced. "Was easier than we thought," Jade said, "but then we did have the PTP that was located in the most remote part of Genesia. Very little security and easy to overpower them". The two had a sense of accomplishment about them.

"Been a while since we've had a chance to kick some ass," Rae smiled at her sister.

Varian and Nemar arrived next and, of course, I jumped in the pit, threw my arms around him, gave him a big kiss.

Nemar snickered, "He missed you too."

Finally, Lynn and Baxor showed up. Baxor looked a little beat up, but he was healing quickly.

"What happened?" Valan asked.

"Added security - had to fight a few off. Killed two of them," he answered.

"I think I did my part too," Lynn said, with an

indignant tone, "you didn't do everything yourself you know."

Another flash. We all turned to see who it could be. Baxor stepped closer, "Mother?"

"Hello son," she greeted, "and how nice of you to have dinner ready for me." She started toward me, then stopped, "It's you."

"How are you here?" I asked.

"I waited for my moment and it came as soon as I saw you with this joined human," she looked to her son, "Nice idea, blowing up the PTP. I hardly made it out in time, but you know it won't slow them down for long. Now, I'm hungry, time to eat," I stepped back and Varian stepped in front of me, "Oh don't worry, my dear, I won't make that mistake again. Perhaps another day when we can talk one on one," she bared her fangs, "We'll catch up another day son. That is, if you're still alive. Goodbye."

"What did that comment mean?"

Bax sighed, "Mom never was very maternal, found me more of a burden, really, unless she could use me as a pawn against my father, but that's a long story. I think what she really means is assassins are already here and on the move. We are being hunted. The only good thing is, they could have landed anywhere and it will take a while to search for or find us," he said.

"Not much of a comfort," I countered.

Lynn approached with a compact in her hand, "This may give you some comfort at least. Look," she ordered, holding up the mirror.

ON THE RUN

Once again, we all decided to go our separate ways. May as well make it difficult to be found. As long as I stayed with Varian, I was happy and I was back to my old self, age-wise, that is. Valan was right, give it a few days for my body to correct itself, adjust to home.

Everyone went in opposite directions with the

condition that we not contact one another for at least two weeks. That would give us time to blend into the population. I mean, really, with seven billion people on the planet, all shapes and sizes it should be easy, right?

Varian and I decided to find Hugh Morgan. When I told Varian I wasn't able to find him, he thought it best we go see if he was still safe or even at the same place we left him.

Back at Hugh's hide-a-way, we discovered the reason we couldn't get a hold of him. Two assassins were going through the building, checking every nook and cranny, closet, even looking for secret levers that would open a hidden passage. These guys were thorough. Varian watched and listened to them talking between each other. They seemed angry, frustrated at not finding what they were looking for.

He saw the security cameras, '*He saw them coming and ran. Good.*' he thought.

"Are you the one they call Varian Kanor?"

Varian turned to find a watcher a few feet away and closing in, "Sorry, you've got the wrong one," he lied.

The watcher bared his weapons, "I don't think so,"

he struck him so hard I could hear a loud crack; he flew back and hit the cement sidewalk hard. An attack like that would have killed a human, but these were Genesians. I jumped out from the hedge I was hiding behind, my .38 drawn, "Hey, asshole?" I yelled.

"Carlynn, no!"

The watcher turned and laughed loudly, "A human. You think that little cap gun will stop me? I think a snack is in order."

I fired the first shot right between his eyes. It knocked him down but didn't stop him and yeah, he was pissed when he got up. I saw my aim was dead on but the hole was closing fast. I aimed again and fired. Dead hit, right in the chest. He fell. Is he dead? I ran up to him, '*Looks dead. Wow it worked,*' I thought, mentally giving myself a pat on the back.

"Don't get excited yet," Varian said as he approached the watcher, who, I noticed, was still breathing! Incredible! Couldn't be. I hit the heart, I know I did.

"There's only one way, Carlynn."

I realized what he meant and this time I turned my

back. It was enough I shot him.

Varian finished the job, took my hand and we started walking away when he asked, "What kind of bullets are you using and when did you learn to shoot?"

"Armor-piercing bullets and my father taught me to shoot when I was ten."

"He's a good teacher."

"Hey, the student wasn't so bad either."

We both laughed.

"Citizen!"

Varian froze, "Shit", he whispered, "get ready."

"Ready for what?"

"Citizen. Stay where you are. Do not move," the voice called out, "Failure to obey will result in death."

"Now!" Varian scooped me up into his arms and ran. "Where are we going?" I called out not sure he heard. I was sure I heard footsteps following us. It could only be the assassins. '*Dammit!*'

I hoped Varian carrying me didn't slow him down too much. I didn't want to be the reason we got caught. One thing was perfectly clear, we were now on the run.

Wonder how the others were doing?

Hey! How are you doing? Yes, it's me, Carlynn Willows. When last you heard from me, Varian and I were on the run with a couple of assassins hot on our heels, literally.

I am happy to report the two assassins are dead and here's how:

"You still have that .38?"

"Yes of course."

"Take it out and start shooting!"

"You're running too fast. I can't see them!"

"Guess."

"But…"

"Carlynn, just shoot. You might hit one of them. Enough to slow them down."

I drew the pistol and started firing at the blurred figures hoping like hell I'd hit one or maybe both. It worked. I hit both, one in the abdomen and the other in the groin. *'Ouch,'* I thought instinctively. They were down and Varian had to act fast. I didn't actually see him do it but the end result was him standing over two bodies, a heart in each hand and large holes in the chests of the dead Genesians.

"You ok, babe?"

"Yeah," he answered, "just wish it didn't have to be this way."

"Me too."

"We'd better get rid of the bodies. First a watcher and now two assassins, the judges would have a hay day with my indiscretions."

"Hay day? You're picking up Earth lingo quickly," I

said.

He smiled, "Come on, let's get this over with."

We buried the bodies quickly and moved on. Our mission to find Hugh Morgan still top priority.

"Do you ever get tired of carrying me?" I asked as we raced, Varian had me in him arms again. Not that I was complaining but my usual insecurities crept in, you know, *'Am I too heavy,'* one of the things our society still focused on, especially with women.

He seemed to sense my uneasiness, "Not at all. I quite enjoy it," he gave me a quick kiss.

"Where are we going?"

"I have a feeling I know where Hugh is," he answered and when we stopped, I saw the institute again.

"You're kidding."

"Nope. I'm guessing he's underground again."

We walked in the front doors, "Welcome to CASI," a middle aged woman, impeccably dressed, hair perfectly coifed in a French roll, sitting behind a large, half-moon shaped desk greeted, "How can I help you?"

I scanned the area, the whole place was cleaned up and back in action, "When did this happen?" I asked her.

"When did what happen? I'm sorry, I just started working here," she said, "What can I help you with?"

"Is Hugh Morgan here?" Varian asked.

"Yes he is. One moment please."

We sat in the waiting area a few minutes when Hugh came out to see us.

"Carlynn, Varian, good to see you! How have you been? You're looking well," he greeted, with too much joy in his voice. This was not the Hugh I knew. Our dual expression of disdain evident, making him shift his stance. He was nervous.

"Um, follow me into the boardroom. Coffee is ready and I'd love to have a chat," he said, his tone was enough to tell me this was a show he was putting on.

We followed him into the room, he shut the door, "Please, have a seat."

"I'll stand, thanks. What's going on Hugh?" I asked; more like demanded.

"This is big, Carlynn, I mean really big. I mean as on a global scale," he said.

"I know, believe me."

"Government funding is responsible for getting

C.A.S.I. up and running again and in exchange, we work for them. They are working with them, Carlynn. World leaders are working together with the Genesians! They've known for some time of their existence. How and when they arrived. We are to help develop the blood substitute they require," he explained.

"This is an archeological institute, not a lab."

"On the surface, yes, but the main purpose is to develop the new blood substitute."

"There is none," Varian informed, "You've been fooled. What's coming is an invasion, Hugh. There's nothing friendly about it."

"No, no you're wrong. They said..."

"They lied."

"Hugh, Varian is telling the truth. I don't know what the powers that be told you, but I was there. I traveled to Genesia and back. I know some of the key vampires connected to this so-called plan; we are all being raised like cattle and will be slaughtered in the end. Earth is a farm for Genesia. Are you listening?"

Hugh was speechless, started shifting from one foot to the other, wringing his hands.

"Are you ok?" I asked, "Have you heard anything I've said?"

"Yeah, yeah," he replied, "I'm sorry. I have to go..."

Just then six security guards burst in and surrounded us, "What the hell!" I yelled.

"I'm so sorry," Hugh apologized and left the room.

Varian's weapons were out, "You're no match for me," he warned.

"They may not be, but I am," Baya walked in, "Now you will behave, Varian, or I will kill Carlynn and send you back home to face the judges. Oh and these guns are equipped with ammunition that can kill you, believe me. I designed them myself."

I looked at Varian, hoping he could sense what I wanted from him. He moved his head slightly, 'No.' My stare grew more intense. I threw my arms around him, "I'm so afraid Varian. What will we do?" I feigned a sob.

"It's ok, Carlynn, we'll get through this together," he said, convincingly.

Baya laughed, "Isn't this sweet."

"Yeah, sweet," I echoed, "...bitch." Varian jumped up and over the security, knocked two of them down, grabbed the gun and aimed at Baya's head. I moved quickly behind him.

"My turn," he said, "tell your entourage to back off. We're leaving."

"You're faster than I thought, Varian. You won't get far," she hissed.

"We'll take our chances," I hissed back.

We backed out of the room, Varian scooped me up again and headed for the front doors. A loud bang rang out, Varian stumbled but continued on. Once again, I had no idea where we were going since my eyes could not focus quickly enough at the fast moving landscape going by at a dizzying speed.

We finally stopped. Actually, we fell and I tumbled. When I got up, I saw him down, "Varian!" I ran over to him, turned his body over onto his back and saw the large hole in his side, "How? What do I do?" panic setting in, "Tell me."

"I'm healing already, don't worry," he said.

"Not fast enough. I thought you said nothing can hurt you here."

"I guess Baya made some improvements to your

Earth ammo....ahhhh!" he winced.

"Ok, I'm going to guess that you need this," I offered my wrist.

"No, I'm fine, or I will be."

"Don't argue, just do it. You're bleeding out too fast. The twins showed you how, so…" my wrist half an inch from his mouth still ready, I closed my eyes and braced myself.

There was virtually no pain. I mean, I felt a very brief sting, like that of a bee, but it subsided almost instantly. To be honest, I felt almost as if I was in a trance of sorts. I found myself staring off into the distance, but saw nothing. No trees, leaves, grass or open fields, just oblivion, I couldn't even think.

When Varian finished I came back to the real world and instantly checked his wound, which was gone, completely healed. I didn't know if I'd ever get used to that. I was still reeling because my life had been turned upside down in a very short period of time!

We sat for a while, recuperating, something I insisted on, being he almost died, in my opinion. He argued he was fine, didn't need to rest and that we should keep moving but I insisted. I had to admit, I needed to take a break. I'd never been involved with a man, or vampire, and the surprises kept coming. My mind was going a million miles an hour; no sign of slowing down. *'What are we going to do now?'*

"Var.."

"Shhht."

"Don't you..."

"Carlynn," he whispered, "we're not alone."

I swallowed my oncoming protest at his shhh(ing) me and looked around slowly, not that I could spot any intruder the same way Varian could.

"Come out, I know you're there."

43

A man stepped out into the open. The open being a small glen, hidden amongst a thick forest as far as I could see.

He was tall like Varian, with dark curly hair, shorter cut but some curls fell on his forehead. Pale complexion, an obvious Genesian, with those dark almost black eyes that seemed to bore right through you. He was handsome, but not ruggedly handsome. His features were softer, a slightly rounder chin, larger eyes, almost baby-faced yet not. He was wearing a worn leather jacket with a t-shirt underneath, dark jeans, and hiking boots.

"Who are you?" Varian asked.

"I'm Kaleg Augustus. Who are you?"

"Varian Kanor and this is Carlynn Willows."

The stranger circled us several times, not saying a word, just staring at us. I was becoming uneasy and Varian was beginning to get angry, "What are you doing?" I demanded.

"I am sorry, you remind me of my wife...she died", he answered.

"Oh, I'm sorry."

"Forgive me, I don't mean to be rude but it's been a while since I've seen a fellow Genesian and I'm very surprised to see one cavorting with a human. It's not 'normal' by our standards..."

He stepped closer and bared his weapons, "Hold it stranger," Varian moved in front of me, "Oh no you don't."

"Is she not with you because you intend to feed? I thought I could join you."

"No, she isn't, back off. She's a friend, not food."

"Very well," he sat on the ground.

"How long have you been here and why are you here?" Varian was beginning to remind me of me, I was usually the one to ask the questions.

"Many, many years. Approximately three thousand or so, I was sent here as an assassin."

We backed away immediately, intending to run, when he said, "Please, don't go. I have not carried out my role as an assassin for two thousand of those years. I found it tedious and very unfulfilling. The judges don't know as they seem to have forgotten about me."

"How can they forget about you? Don't you have to 'check in' with them occasionally? They must know that you haven't been in contact and may have sent more to find you."

"Well, they haven't. I've lived quite peacefully here so far and I intend to keep it that way. Perhaps they will remember I'm here one day."

Varian and Kaleg continued to talk as I drifted off, thinking of the idea of living three thousand years. The history one would experience and witness. Then there was the downside of losing loved ones, watching everyone you care about leave you, permanently…

My mind got foggy for a moment, then it seemed to fade and a picture was before me. I saw a large palace with huge marble columns, almost as white as fresh fallen snow, the whole thing shone in the sunlight.

People mulling around the front of the palace, some gathered in small groups talking amongst themselves, all dressed in linens. Linens…as in togas? Roman style attire…the image faded to another inside the palace. I'm not sure how I knew it was in fact inside, I just knew.

It was 38AD and the newest ruler of Rome had ruled for just one year and that ruler was known as Caligula.

This first year of rule was a happy one for all of Rome. Their new emperor was kind, generous, the people loved him. Then something happened…he changed, became cruel, violent, a man that the people were beginning to fear. He'd have people killed for no apparent reason, purely for his enjoyment, had large parties with all the diplomats and their wives who he decided were his to use any way he saw fit. No one would oppose him for fear of execution.

A woman lay on a large marble bench that was draped in red satin cloth and large plump pillows, one of which the woman clutched tightly in her arms. She was scared, but why?

A man entered the room, "Ah, Junia. I am so happy to see you," the man said, but I couldn't see his face. Junia didn't answer him.

"Now, my dear, don't be that way. I have left you alone for some time and used others to satisfy my thirst, but today I cannot stay away any longer. I hunger for you."

She spoke, "Why me? There are so many that will do anything you ask of them. Take them as they are happy to please you."

"But I am happiest when I am with you."

"I am not. You repulse me."

"You don't have a choice and its comments such as that that will garner punishment," he said as he approached the bench and slapped her face, "You will submit."

She pushed her face into the pillow hoping the softness would soothe the burn of the slap. It felt like he broke her jaw; she could feel the swelling. She kept the pillow over her face as he bent down, lay on top of her, found her neck, and sunk his teeth into the soft flesh. The room was silent, except for his occasional moan as he sucked for what seemed like hours. It was like watching a movie in slow motion. When he finally stopped, he got up and I saw her move. I was so relieved she was alive.

He turned to leave and he saw me, he actually saw me. How do I know? He smiled at me and said, "Hello, Carlynn."

I jerked.

"Carlynn," Varian's voice brought me out of my trance.

"Yes."

"Are you ok? You looked so far away."

"I'm fine. Daydreaming, I guess."

I felt his arm around my shoulder, he kissed my forehead and I leaned into him. I was falling hard for this man. Safe, I was safe, I thought.

I looked at Kaleg and asked him, "Have we met?"

"I don't think so, Carlynn," he answered, "I'm sure I would have remembered you."

"Yeah, ok. You look familiar to me."

"I'm sure you are mistaken," he said, but his smile

was not friendly in my opinion.

I knew this man, but how and where had I met him before? I had to have met him before, hadn't I? I mean, I saw him in my vision, my deja vu. I'm not even sure it was deja vu; a past life perhaps, if there is such a thing. Many people believed they'd lived many lives over, maybe they were right. Maybe I'd lived many lives and this was one of them, which would mean that my meeting Varian was not the first time I'd encountered a Genesian but the second time and if I'd met Kaleg in a past life. Who's to say I hadn't met more throughout the ages. This could be a human's kind of immortality. I mean, if Genesians lived for thousands or even millions of years, they were virtually immortal and if we were in fact their creation, then being reborn was our immortality. It could be how they started out too and evolved through time to what they were now. So maybe all the times I'd experienced feelings of deja vu were me remembering a past life. Great, more crap I had to think through, as if I didn't have enough on my mind at that point.

"Carlynn," Varian caught my attention again.

"Yes."

"We have to get moving. We'll go a little farther than usual to avoid being found by Baya and her cronies."

"What do you have in mind?"

"You'll see," he smirked.

"You're up to something."

"It was nice to meet you, Kaleg, but we'll have to be going now. Good luck," Varian said.

"Farewell, my new friends," he bid us goodbye and was gone.

Varian turned to me, "Ok, what was that all about? It's like you were on another planet, zoned out."

"You pick up our lingo very quickly. Interesting how you use 'another planet' too."

"Don't change the subject, talk."

"It's silly."

"Let me decide what's silly."

I told him of my 'vision' that Kaleg was in it, he was actually the Roman emperor, Caligula, the type of ruler he turned out to be, how he fed on this Junia woman and she lived, "It's obvious he figured out how to feed without killing long before Rae and Jade and their parents. What I don't understand is why I saw this."

He listened intently.

"And, Caligula was killed by his own guards in the end. How is Kaleg even alive if he is actually Caligula?" I concluded.

"Quite the vision," Varian responded, "but I don't think it's anything, really. Put it out of your mind," we stood and he pulled me close, "Come on, I know a place we can blend in and have a little fun."

"Where are we going?"

"Always with the questions!" he laughed, "It's a surprise."

Within minutes, we were at the Winnipeg airport, awaiting a flight I was not prepared for at all. No luggage meant no clothes, toiletries, and no cash. Well, I had my debit card of course, and luckily for me, I always carried my passport. You never know when you'll be sent to a foreign country and this was just such an occasion.

Varian assured me not to worry about the small stuff as we could buy everything we needed when we got to our destination, Vegas!

Our flight was uneventful. Varian scanned the entire plane to be sure no other Genesians were there so I could relax if only for a couple of hours. I slept the whole time. I didn't realize how tired I was until I awoke as the plane touched the tarmac. As we deplaned, I leaned against Varian, trying to wake up fully.

We took a chauffeur-driven car to our hotel, the Venetian. Interesting choice, I must admit, but when Varian asked where we should stay, it came out with no hesitation. He raised an eyebrow and said, "I see."

I felt I had to explain, "It's the one Lynn and I wanted to stay at when we would go together. We'd always planned to come here for a girl's weekend some time. Just never got around to it. She's going to be pissed when she finds out I went without her."

The sight of Vegas at night was spectacular. So many lights, the water and light show in front of the Bellagio, Paris with the Eiffel tower, the Luxor in the shape of the pyramid, I could kick myself for not mentioning the Luxor instead of the Venetian. So many to choose from, all beautiful and full of people having the times of their lives, gambling, going to the shows and attractions, not to mention the shopping. For a moment I was sad to think that this could be short-lived if the judges of Genesia had their way.

"This will kill Lynn when she finds out," I whispered.

"Don't worry about that," Varian heard my whisper, "she and Kaeton could have been here already. You never know."

"Ah, no way, I'll kill her!"

"Relax," he laughed, "just a suggestion. She could have and not told you, worrying about the same consequences you're thinking of."

"You have a point."

"Just saying."

"Yeah, yeah. Ok, star boy, let's find our room and then do a little shopping for the basics."

The Venetian. An absolutely massive hotel with stone pillars, a water way and gondolas, complete with gondoliers, singing as they row along, palm trees, and the detailed carving on each wall, inside and out. All reminiscent of ancient Italy, without being there. I thumbed through a brochure I picked up at the check-in counter and looked through it while Varian was checking us in, and saw this picture of a gondola rowing around what looked like Venice, only instead of homes, chateaus, small shops, and docks, it was a modern shopping mall. It didn't take away from the ambiance in any way. I made up my mind I would convince Varian to take a ride on this boat while we were here. I mean, may as well take in the atmosphere right?

A tap on my shoulder. Varian held up the room keys and motioned for us to find our room, but first, we had to find our way through the casino.

The casino was a sight. The bright lights, bells ringing, VLTs as far as the eye could see and a sea of people to navigate through. We arrived on a Thursday, which meant the weekend crowd was arriving in droves. It also meant the gambling had begun, some playing for the sheer enjoyment, not putting everything on the line, but just having the experience of Vegas and others dropping hundreds, even thousands, hoping for the big payoff. We watched some of them for a while and I could see how one could get lost in the excitement, yet almost pity the ones thinking they will win big. I watched one gentleman sit at a video slot machine, putting in twenty dollar bills for the first few minutes, then pull out some one hundred dollar bills and start using those. He may have been well-to-do or not; you couldn't tell these days. He didn't look as though he could afford to lose that kind of cash but as the few minutes moved on, he lost it all, got up, headed for an ATM and withdrew a handful of cash. We decided to move on, but as I glanced over my shoulder I saw him sit back down at the same machine, and I swear I saw a tear stream down his cheek.

We got off the elevator on the fourth floor, found our room and went in. It wasn't just a room; it was a suite. A large, king size bed made up to perfection, a lounger at the foot of it. A night stand on either side in beautiful, dark pine, a large plush recliner only a few feet away from the lounger, looking almost as comfortable as the bed.

A sunken living room again with a sectional you could lose yourself in and next to it, a small dining area complete with table and four chairs. A large chandelier above the table that lit up just enough so that it gave an impression of an intimate dining experience.

"Wow," I said.

"Let's get cleaned up a bit and go."

"Ok."

I splashed some warm water on my face, ran a brush through my hair, trying hard not to look like I'd been through a wringer in the last 24 hours. Varian cleaned up in minutes. I secretly resented that, he could look so good with very little effort.

We left the hotel and started walking and walking and walking...Vegas was one place where comfortable shoes was a must and I needed better ones. We stopped at a Walgreens and I picked up the basic necessities, shampoo, conditioner, toothpaste, etc.

Our next stop was a dress shop, which I didn't really care for too much. I'm not much of a dress person but Varian insisted I get a couple of evening dresses for special evenings on the town. His words, not mine. I gave in and picked out two – one of them was a typical little black dress with a sweetheart neckline, clean straight lines, the hem just above the knee.

"You'll need new shoes," Varian said

"Runners won't do?" I teased.

He smiled as he picked out the second dress, more fancy than anything I'd ever seen and silver. It shone, "Oh, that's beautiful, but too much, Varian."

"Nothing's too much for you."

"When would I wear this?"

"We'll find an occasion. Try it on."

I tried on the dress, more like a gown, material soft and shimmering, that seemed to flow down to the floor, then rumple at the bottom, "I'm too short for it."

"We'll get some appropriate shoes, Carlynn. You look amazing!"

I sighed.

We left the shop, but not before Varian gave the saleswoman instructions to have the dresses delivered to our hotel room later the same day.

More shopping ahead of us.

When we finally arrived back at the room, we found that someone had been in it. We found two garment bags on the bed with a letter carefully placed on one. We put our bags down and I opened the envelope, "It's an invitation. Looks like all the guests are invited and the clothing, or costumes, are provided."

"Well, let's see what kind of costumes they are," Varian said and opened the first one, "A toga. You've got to be kidding."

I opened the other, "No, they're not," as I pulled the second from the bag, "Wait, there's more," I reached in the bag and pulled out a mask, "Is this normal?" I held up a mask with a handle, more like a stick, and put it to my face.

"It appears it's some kind of masquerade ball," he said and read over the invitation again, "we can either hold the masks to our faces all night or use the string to tie them on."

"I don't know about this, Varian."

"We came to blend in and have a little fun," he said, "Let's go and if we don't like it, we can leave."

I agreed, adjourned to the powder room to start getting ready.

It felt heavenly to stand under a waterfall shower and let the world wash away, if only for a few moments. Once I toweled off, it was business as usual with the beauty routine, drying the hair and putting it into a do that was appropriate for the masquerade, adding the makeup and finally, donning the toga provided. I emerged from the bathroom, "Tada!" Varian stood in costume, ready to go and applauded, "Bravo!"

"Wait, how did you get ready so fast? Maybe I don't want to know."

"I went to another room and before you can ask, it was vacant. I wanted to give you some time to relax and get ready. If I'd joined you, well..."

"I wouldn't have minded, you know."

Varian pulled me close and kissed me softly, "Let's go for a walk on the strip. Kill some time."

"Like this?" I looked at my costume and his.

"This is Vegas. No one will care. Come on, we have time."

We walked through the congested casino to the exit. I noticed some people were in costume already, masks on and using their extra time to try their luck. We left the hotel and ran down the steps, over the bridge of the river; I noticed the gondoliers were busy.

"I really want a ride on that yet."

"We will."

Walking down the crowded strip was entertaining,

to say the least. People from around the world came to Vegas for the gambling, sights and shows. We weren't out of place in our garb at all. There were street entertainers, men and women handing out their cards for the local clubs, dance and strip alike, the water fountain show that came on every half hour was beautiful and we happened to see it just as the new show started.

It was so fun just people-watching too. Some in shorts and tops, others dressed to the nines, some very casual and relaxed, and then there were the panhandlers. There was definitely no shortage of those in the city. I did, however, resent how some used pets to tug at people's hearts to give a little something. One can't help it, you feel so sorry for those poor animals out there with their owners all day long in the scorching sun and heat. We hopped the bus and I noticed one of the panhandlers that I saw on the street with his kitten hopped on right after us, his kitten safely in a kitty kennel. It made me wonder, as I'd heard of people making a fairly good living on the street. Of course, that was not the case for all people on the streets of Vegas. We saw one man go by, dressed in army fatigues, filthy, unkempt, and hardly able to walk. I looked down and saw he had no shoes on, his feet red, swollen full of open sores.

"Varian, I can't let him go without giving him something. Please."

"Ok, babe. He's a veteran and needs someone." He went after the fallen hero, stopped him to talk for a moment and handed him some money. I could see the man's eyes tear up as he thanked Varian for the help. I overheard Varian tell the man where we were staying and that if he needed, he could come to the front of the hotel and ask for him. The man looked at him in disbelief as he walked back to rejoin me.

"Thank you for doing that,"

"I remember my father telling me of the treatment of our veterans on Genesia. Years ago, in our history, many of ours were treated badly as well. They had many of the same problems as yours do here, such as post-traumatic stress. That's what it is here, right?" I nodded. "My father told me that no matter how I felt about war, always treat the men and women who fight for us with respect and gratitude."

"I thought you didn't have these kinds of conflicts on Genesia anymore."

"We don't and I am glad I wasn't around to see any of it. My parents were and they didn't paint a pretty or glamorous picture. He wanted me to know what it was like and never forget."

I really wanted that in our world, but I suppose we haven't evolved enough yet. "Do you mind me asking how much you gave him?" I asked.

"No I don't mind. A lot, I wanted him off the streets and to get some help. I could tell he really needed it and found out he had no one else to help him. Now, let's make our way back to the hotel. I'm sure the party has started already."

I smiled at the warm-hearted man I fell for and took his hand.

We saw more costumed people as we walked back, "Must be a monster costume ball in one of the other casinos," I observed. There were people dressed as mummies, Frankenstein and Dracula. I glanced over at Varian when I saw the latter and noticed his expression of complete disdain. I giggled a bit. "Ha, ha, very funny," he said.

"You have to be able to laugh at yourself as well,

Varian."

Then I thought I saw a familiar face, dressed as Dracula. Was that Kaleg? Couldn't be. I decided it was my imagination and I put it out of my mind, but I couldn't. As I looked around some more, I saw more people in costume who looked like they were Genesian. The dark hair, dark eyes, the pale skin, I was sure it wasn't makeup. I wondered if Varian noticed it, he had to. He said he could feel when another Genesian was close by, so he had to know.

"Varian," my voice quivered a bit.

"I know," he whispered, "pretend you don't notice."

I turned my attention elsewhere, pretending to enjoy the sights, secretly scared to death. We ducked behind a vendor, and he picked me up and we took off. It was so fast no one would notice, no human at least. Before I could catch my breath, we were back at the hotel, masks on and walked into the ballroom.

45

The ballroom was filled to capacity with people dressed in togas and masks covering their faces. If you didn't stick to your escort, or forgot what mask they were wearing, there was a good chance you'd lose them in the crowd, which is exactly what happened to me. Wanting something to drink, Varian offered to get it for me. He left me at one of the roulette tables, asking me not to move around as he may not be able to find me again. I laughed and said, "Might be fun, you trying to figure which one is me!"

It was fun watching gamblers bet their lucky numbers and be happy to lose miserably. The whole gala was a benefit ball so every dollar the casino took in went straight to charity. After chatting with one of the cocktail waitresses for a moment, I found that the entire staff had agreed to donate their time and I was glad Varian and I decided to attend.

The band started. Many grabbed their partners and headed for the dance floor. I wondered how many of them actually danced with their significant others. Maybe it didn't matter, the idea was to have fun and give to charity. There was a tap on my shoulder; I turned to see Varian with a champagne glass. I took a sip and he motioned for us to dance. I obliged.

We twirled around the dance floor a few times and I commented how graceful he was. I felt like I had two left feet. I had no idea how to ballroom dance and tried my best to follow his lead. I could see a half smile beneath a mask that covered most of his face, but something was not quite right. It looked like him, yet didn't.

ANCIENT ORIGINS: GENERATIONS

Varian pounded on the door that had him locked in a vault with a three-foot-thick steel door. He cursed himself for being so naïve. He'd been lured to the basement of the casino on the premise that someone had been hurt by one of the heavy carts used to move the stacks of cash to the vaults, and needed help until the paramedics arrived. On reflection, he realized it was a feeble excuse and he really had to work on being such a trusting person. For a second he smirked at the 'trusting person' thought; it made him think of himself in human form, something he wasn't. Then it was back to the task at hand, getting out of the vault, finding Kaleg and kicking his ass. He knew it was Kaleg because as the vault closed he smiled at him. It's safe to say he wasn't getting out through the door, as much as he tried, all he could manage was a few dents. The vault door was too thick, so he moved to the walls. As he suspected, this was easier to penetrate.

After three more dances around the dance floor I knew this wasn't Varian and even if I couldn't see his face,

I knew it had to be Kaleg. Not knowing what to do or how to get away from him, I managed to keep a smile on my face and not alert him to my being aware. A few more spins, he asked if I was having fun, and I nodded, but had no control of my answer, "Yes, Gauis Julius Caesar Augustus Germanicus."

I froze, 'Where did that come from?' was the question I asked myself. Kaleg's smile disappeared in an instant, "What did you call me?"

I decided not to show fear, "You heard me, or should I have said Caligula? You really thought you could fool me? Please." My mouth was going, filter turned off; I couldn't seem to stop myself.

"That name, how did you know?" he demanded an answer.

We were the only two in a crowd of people not dancing at this point, "I don't know," I answered and I really didn't know; it just came out.

"I always hated that bloody nickname!"

Ok, he was really angry and there was no way I could defend myself against him. I searched the crowd, desperately looking for Varian, *'Where are you?'* I whispered.

"He's safely locked away," Kaleg answered.

"Not anymore," Varian was behind him, "You overlooked the thickness of the casino walls. Eighteen-inch-thick brick is easy to break through, mind you, security is now locking everything down as they think someone broke in to steal their cash."

Kaleg was not amused, "You are a problem, aren't you? No matter," and Varian was gone. The loud crash of one of the refreshment tables smashing to pieces alerted me to him. Kaleg threw him almost across the room. In a split second, Varian grabbed Kaleg and the fight continued. It must have been vicious as things started flying, the gaming tables were crashing together, cards littered the air almost like a ticker tape parade and floated down to the floor, the roulette round rolled by me. I decided to move to the wall instead of the middle of the floor. As the mayhem continued, the guests started screaming and yelling, fear of not being able to see what was causing the destruction, driving them to the hotel doors, which were locked. Security had locked them as they searched for potential robbers, but this didn't stop the people from pushing, kicking, and throwing chairs, anything they could get their hands on to break the glass, bust open the doors and escape. They succeeded.

I slipped away and ran to back to the room. *'It has to be here,'* I frantically searched, *'I swear I took it with me.'* I reached into my jacket pocket, *'Aha!'*

I ran back to the ballroom; it looked more like a battle field. They were still fighting. I tried my best to follow them around the room but it was difficult, *'If they'd only stay still for just a second,'* I thought. Every time I thought I could get a lock on Kaleg, he disappeared. They both did and ended up at the other end of the room. Then a cymbal from the stage where the band played rolled by. *'Come on, stop moving.'* Kaleg stopped just a few feet before me and winked, *'Bang.'* Varian was now in front of me blocking my view, neither one moved. Varian slowly turned to me, letting me see what happened, I hit my target, "How?" Varian asked.

"I managed to swipe one." I answered and held up one of the guns I took when we escaped from Baya.

Kaleg's shoulder was mangled. Skin hung down in shreds, blood spewed and I could see the white of the bone. It had a large hole that seemed to be getting smaller. He was healing. Dammit!

Kaleg's reaction to my assault was that of complete surprise on his part. His eyes were wide, black and I swear there was fear there.

"How is this possible?" he asked

"Courtesy of Baya Kan," I answered.

"It's been many years since I've heard that name, Baya wife of Balan."

"Yes," Varian said, "she modified some of Earth's weapons, more specifically, the ammunition. You are lucky Carlynn hit your shoulder and not your heart."

"When did this happen?"

"Don't know for certain, but it happened."

"I take it this fight is over," I interjected.

"For now, my dear," Kaleg said, "I need to heal faster and for that I will need to take my leave of you. Unless you want to help me," he took a step toward me, Varian stood in his way, "I see I'm on my own," and with that, he left.

I breathed a sigh of relief.

"We have to leave. Let's get back to the room,"

Varian said.

The ballroom was a disaster area and I really didn't want to be found here where there would be a lot of questions asked. Questions I couldn't answer and the police sirens were getting louder.

Back at the room I plopped on the bed, "Will I ever have a normal day again?"

"What's normal to you?"

"You know, wake up, have a cup of coffee, get ready and head off to work."

"Ah, I see." Varian had a tone of sadness and I realized I may have given the impression that everything that had happened in the past few weeks was his fault.

"This is not your fault Varian."

"But if you hadn't met me..."

"But...I did...and I don't regret it in any way."

He didn't look convinced, "Varian if I hadn't met you, I'd be blind to the future of the human race, still be digging up bones, guessing who they are, what happened to them...and now that I hear myself say it, it all seems like a total waste of time."

"Your work is not a waste of time."

I smiled. Now he was trying to make me feel better. How in the hell can a guy be this nice!

"I never would have met you, Varian, and I can't imagine you not being in my life. I can't...is that too much? I mean, we haven't known each other very long and most guys would run if a woman got close too fast."

Varian grabbed me, pulled me close and kissed me softly. I didn't want it to stop but just as things got more intense, there was a knock at the door.

"Shit," I cursed and answered the door.

"Now, did you really think you could come to Vegas and have fun without me?" Lynn smiled brightly.

"Lynn!" I grabbed her and hugged her tightly.

"How did you find me?"

"Carlynn, you didn't turn off your locator on your cell. Anyone can find you."

"Shit," I cursed again, and searched for my cell amid the mess of clothes lying around that we didn't take the time to clean up. Then a thought came over me, what if the reason I saw those other vampires on the street earlier that evening was because we were followed and all because of my stupid cell phone. Arg! 'You idiot.'

I found the phone in the washroom beside the sink and immediately opened the settings menu, turned off all locations. Not that it would do any good now, but I secretly hoped for the best. Maybe the best would be to destroy the phone...

Varian, Lynn and Kaeton ran into the washroom when they heard a smash, "What happened?" Lynn asked.

I held up what was left of my cell in one hand and a shoe in the other, "I decided it's for the best."

"Going off the grid, nice," Kaeton said as he grabbed the remote and body slammed himself onto the bed, "Let's see what's on." He'd turned into one of those guys who channel surfed, ugh, like watching my father. After a long day on the fields, trying desperately to make a go of growing barley, he'd come in, eat supper and proceed to the lazyboy. He'd sit down with an audible loud sigh, grab the remote and go through the channels over and over until he'd finally find something watchable. Usually the news and after all the surfing I'd always ask, "If you just wanted the news, why do you go through so many times?" and his answer would always be, "To see what's on, honey," then he'd snicker.

Kaeton was no better. He finally settled on, yep you guessed it, a news channel. The first thing I we saw was the headline, 'Breaking News.'

"Hey guys. Shut up for a minute. Check this out," I said.

'A spectacular event never seen before. Scientists connected with SETI, together with NASA and astronomers in charge of the Hubble Telescope announced today that we will witness a meteor shower unlike anything we have ever seen before.'

They went on to say that a cluster of meteors was headed our way, experts unable to say whether it would hit us or just pass by. At this point it was a wait and see scenario.

Varian grabbed the remote and switched the TV off, "We know that they've repaired the PTPs. I have a feeling they are sending Genesians sooner than we thought."

"It's not a meteor shower."

"No."

"Wait, how is it they can see this? I thought..."

"They can't always watch every inch of space, Carlynn. They got lucky and spotted this one. Remember how you thought I was a falling star?"

"Yeah, I do."

"So, what do we do now?" Lynn asked. No one answered as no one had an answer.

I broke the silence, "Varian, I want to go home. I have to see my parents; make sure they're ok."

"Then we will go back," he said.

"So much for us having a fun vacation," Lynn said, "and we just got here."

"You don't have to come, Lynn," I said, "you two can still stay and have some fun. I don't want to be the reason you feel you have to leave."

"We are coming with you and that's that. Besides, it wouldn't be any fun without you."

"Hey!" Kaeton protested.

Lynn laughed, "You know what I mean, babe," she wrapped her arms around him and planted a kiss.

As they were busy locking lips, I dragged Varian into the washroom, closed the door and said, "It might be a good time to do it."

"Do what?"

"You know, the joining thing?"

"Whoa, aren't you getting ahead of yourself? We don't need to do this, Carlynn."

"But..."

"Let's see what we're up against first before we take any drastic measures."

"What do you mean 'drastic measures'? Varian, there's an invasion coming sooner than we expected. How can I defend myself or my family and friends?" I could hear myself getting louder, growing hysterical. He put his arms around me, held me close.

There was a knock at the door, "Everything ok, Carlynn?" I heard Lynn call out.

I regained my composure, "Yes, I'm ok."

"Ok. We have to go soon guys," she said.

We emerged from the washroom hand in hand, "Ok, let's go."

We made our way around the crowd of people in the hotel lobby, avoided the police who were busy asking guests questions about the battle in the ballroom that nobody saw. I was relieved when we stepped outside because, believe it or not, it was quiet, still. Even with all the people walking, walking, walking, all I felt was a calm quiet.

We walked with the masses for a few minutes when I whispered, "So much for the reprieve."

Varian heard me, "What reprieve?"

"Oh, um, I thought we'd have more time, a lot more, you know."

"Yeah I know. Don't worry, Carlynn, humans are stronger and smarter than the judges on Genesia know. They still think of you as mindless, lower life forms and I'd be glad to be the one to tell them they are wrong."

We walked in silence for a few more minutes but I had to bring the topic up again, "Please don't leave me vulnerable."

"We can talk more about it later," he said, "We have time, I assure you."

"Can I help?"

We all turned to see the familiar face.

EPILOGUE

Now you've heard my story so far. Unbelievable, right? Farfetched, ridiculous, outrageous, etc. Hey, I thought the same at first, until it happened to me.

I used to think the idea of UFOs or aliens was quite stupid, really. And then the idea of monsters lurking in the shadows, hiding in closets, or ghouls bursting from graves. Not anymore. The next time I hear any story of aliens or monsters, believe me, I will listen.

The one fact I'm still trying to fathom is 'Vampires from Outerspace.' It sounds like a bad B movie when I think about it – laughable, but what you've read did happen and there's a lot more I have to tell you. Right now, we are concentrating on staying alive.

Being on the run isn't glamorous or exciting. It's scary as hell.

One thing I will tell you, a fact I do know for certain, we are not alone.

Oh, and by the way – there's more to come.

REPRIEVE

"Don't tell me it can't be done!" Balan was furious. The PTPs had been bombed and by his own son. The judges were ready to have him killed too. If he didn't repair the transports, travel to Earth, find his family and kill them, his head would roll. It was the only way he'd be vindicated. The only way he'd be allowed to live.

This was acceptable in his mind. He would have to sacrifice his family for the greater good. He could take a new wife and start over anyway. The thought of a new life with a new family made him feel better about the future. His current wife hated him and his son betrayed him. There was no love lost between them.

The labourers worked around the clock rebuilding the destroyed transport machines. Parts had to be collected from around the globe and those parts weren't cheap. The manufacturers took advantage of Balan's urgency for parts only they could provide.

Right now, the only thing keeping things calm with

the supreme judges was Balan's forethought to send assassins to Earth before the PTPs were destroyed. However, there was no way of knowing how successful they'd been, if at all, as all communication was down as well. And now there were complications with the transports. 'What else can go wrong?' he thought.

One device's coils snapped, another needed uranium, but when the security container was opened, it was empty. These providers would pay for deceiving him.

Testing the others resulted in the death of two of his guards, who volunteered for the first trial run.

Paranoia was growing in Balan's mind, *'There must be a spy in the midst,'* he thought, *'Baxor did this...and Baya, probably working together.'*

He couldn't think clearly anymore, forgetting that his wife and son did not get along well. Truth was, Baya never wanted Baxor, but duty was pressed upon her. A duty she found ridiculously archaic in this day and age. Consequently, Baxor was raised by a nanny service for the most part and he spent much of his younger years vying for his mother's attention. Attention she never gave. Instead, her attitude was always that of indifference toward him.

FIND ME AT:

www.cjbolyne.com

www.facebook.com/CJ.Bolyne

www.twitter.com/cjbolyne

www.ingramcontent.com/pod-product-compliance
Lightning Source LLC
Chambersburg PA
CBHW070831250626
47159CB00003B/735